A GIRL CALLED JUSTICE

THE SPY AT THE WINDOW

ELLY Griffiths

A GIRL CALLED JUSTICE

THE SPY AT THE WINDOW

Quercus

QUERCUS CHILDREN'S BOOKS

First published in Great Britain in 2022 by Hodder & Stoughton

3 5 7 9 10 8 6 4

Text copyright © Elly Griffiths, 2022
Illustration copyright © Nan Lawson, 2022

The moral rights of the author and illustrator have been asserted.

A CIP catalogue record for this book
is available from the British Library.

ISBN 978 1 78654136 9

Printed and bound in Great Britain by
Clays Ltd, Elcograf S.p.A.

The paper and board used in this book
are made from wood from responsible sources.

Quercus Children's Books
An imprint of
Hachette Children's Group
Part of Hodder & Stoughton Limited
Carmelite House
50 Victoria Embankment
London EC4Y 0DZ

An Hachette UK Company
www.hachette.co.uk

www.hachettechildrens.co.uk

For my mother and for all children
who live through war

Note on exams in the 1930s: The School Certificate
was taken at fifteen or sixteen, just like GCSEs today.
You had to pass six subjects to get a certificate. The
Higher School Certificate was taken at eighteen, like
'A' levels.

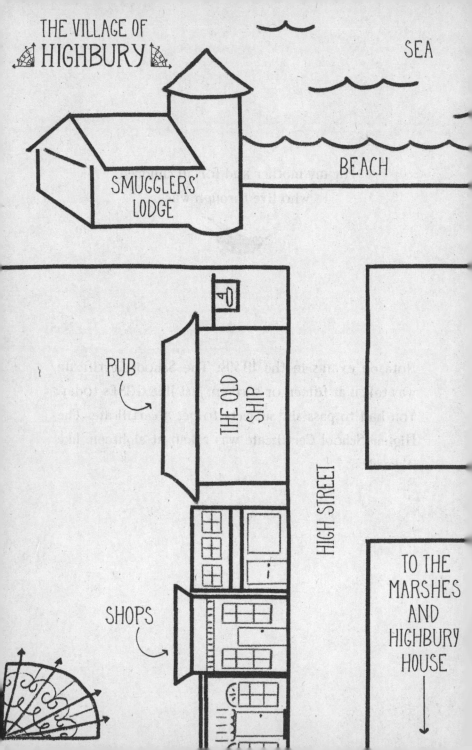

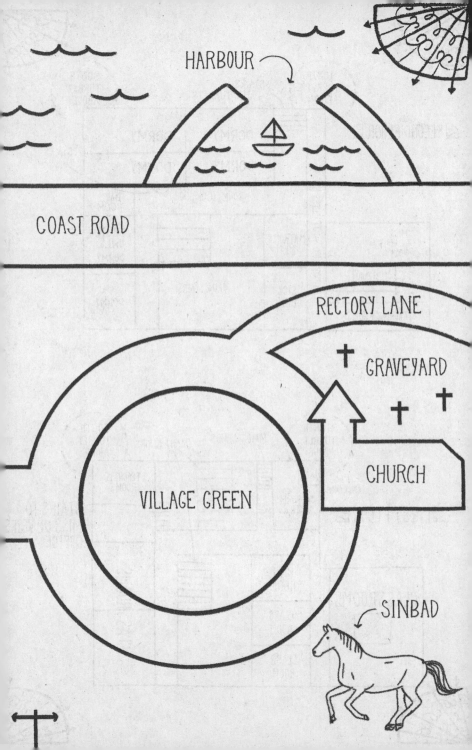

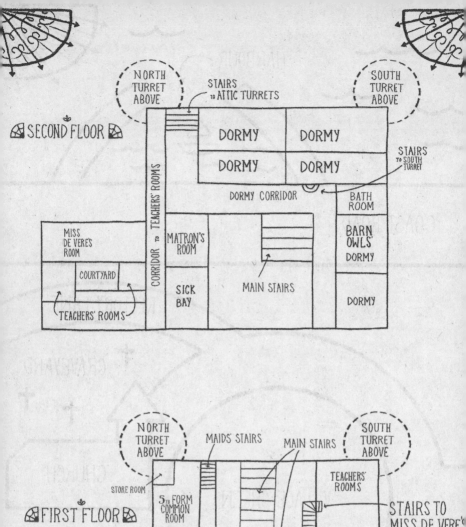

SECOND FLOOR

NORTH TURRET ABOVE

STAIRS TO ATTIC TURRETS

SOUTH TURRET ABOVE

STAIRS TO SOUTH TURRET

DORMY

DORMY

DORMY

DORMY

DORMY CORRIDOR

CORRIDOR TO TEACHERS' ROOMS

BATH ROOM

MISS DE VERE'S ROOM

MATRON'S ROOM

BARN OWLS' DORMY

COURTYARD

SICK BAY

MAIN STAIRS

DORMY

TEACHERS' ROOMS

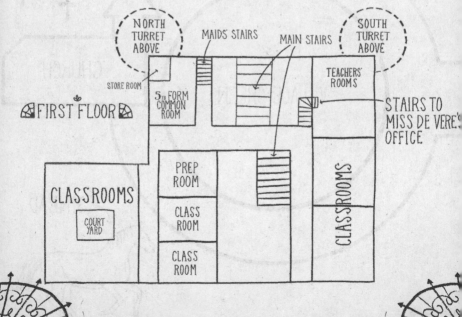

FIRST FLOOR

NORTH TURRET ABOVE

MAIDS' STAIRS

MAIN STAIRS

SOUTH TURRET ABOVE

TEACHERS' ROOMS

STORE ROOM

5TH FORM COMMON ROOM

STAIRS TO MISS DE VERE'S OFFICE

CLASSROOMS

COURT YARD

PREP ROOM

CLASS ROOM

CLASS ROOM

CLASSROOMS

⚘ HIGHBURY HOUSE ⚘

School for the Daughters of Gentlefolk

Staff

Headmistress	— Miss Dolores de Vere
Deputy Headmistress and Latin Mistress	— Miss Brenda Bathurst
Mathematics Mistress	— Miss Edna Morris
English Mistress	— Miss Susan Crane
History Mistress	— Miss Ada Hunting
Science and Cookery Mistress	— Miss Eloise Loomis
Drama and Elocution Mistress	— Miss Joan Balfour
Music and Geography Mistress	— Miss Myfanwy Evans
Games Mistress	— Miss Margaret Heron
Matron	— Mrs Mary O'Brien
Housekeeper	— Mrs Jean Hopkirk
Groundsman and Handyman	— Mr Robert Hutchins

Form 5 at Highbury House

Form Mistress: Miss Heron

Irene Atkins

Letitia Blackstock

Alicia Butterfield

Moira Campbell

Cecilia Delaney

Eva Harris-Brown

Stella Goldman

Joan Kirby

Justice Jones

Flora McDonald

Elizabeth Moore

Freda Saxe-Johnson

Susan Smythe

Rose Trevellian-Hayes

Nora Wilkinson

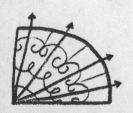

CHAPTER 1

3 *September 1939*

It was funny, thought Justice, how everything could change in an instant. She and Peter were sitting in the garden of her home in London, while Justice's father and Peter's parents listened to the wireless inside. They could hear Prime Minister Neville Chamberlain's voice, sounding very old and weary.

'*This morning the British ambassador in Berlin handed the German government a final note stating that unless we heard from them by eleven o'clock that they were prepared at once to withdraw their troops from Poland, a state of war would exist between us. I have to tell you now that no such undertaking has been received, and that consequently this country is at war with Germany.*'

1

Everything was the same – bees buzzing in the hollyhocks, voices from a neighbouring garden, a bird singing somewhere high above them – but everything had changed.

Peter looked at Justice. 'We're at war,' he said.

It sounded ridiculous. Wars were for history books. Miss Hunting droning on about York and Lancaster. Justice's father had been a pilot in the Great War and had always said that he hoped that she, Justice, would never live through anything similar.

Suddenly, Justice realised that the Great War was now the first world war – and she was going to experience the second.

Inside the grown-ups were talking. Peter's mother, Hilda, was crying. Justice's father, Herbert Jones KC, was using his barrister voice, and sounding very calm and reasonable. Peter's father said something about Czechoslovakia.

Justice didn't want to go into the sitting room, because then it would all be real. She wanted to stay in the garden with Peter. Possibly for ever.

'Will you go back to school?' she asked him. Peter went to a specialist music school in London.

'I suppose so,' he said. 'I heard Mum saying that some London schools would be evacuated. Moved to the countryside.'

Justice's school, Highbury House, was already in the countryside. In fact, it was in the middle of nowhere in Kent, surrounded by marshland and fields. Would Highbury House stay open if there was a war? For years, Justice had dreamt of leaving boarding school but now she thought of her friends Stella, Dorothy and Letitia. Of Nora and Eva too. Even the often insufferable Rose. It would be terrible not to see them again. And she was going into the fifth form in a few weeks, preparing for her School Certificate. She realised that she had even been looking forward to it.

'I hope my school doesn't close,' she said.

'I thought you hated it,' said Peter, who was pacing around the small garden, kicking leaves.

'I thought so too,' said Justice. 'Mind you, nothing will happen immediately.'

At that moment, an air raid siren went off.

It was the most terrifying sound – an awful wail that seemed to echo and reverberate, getting louder and more ominous with every second. Justice and Peter bolted into the house.

'Get your gas masks!' said Hilda. 'Hurry!'

Justice had no idea where she'd left hers. They'd been to get them the other week and Justice had thought they were very scary-looking. The masks for little children were worse.

They were meant to look like Mickey Mouse but, to Justice, they looked like terrifying undersea monsters: bright red rubber with a weird tongue-thing sticking out.

'Should we go to the shelter?' said Hilda. There was an air raid shelter in the communal gardens of the square. It was basically a hole in the ground, with steps leading down. Justice and her father had watched the men digging it.

'Let's all be calm,' said Herbert. 'It might be a false alarm.'

As he said this, another sound filled the air. It was almost as bad as the air raid warning but Herbert said, 'That's the "all clear". Everything's all right.' Hilda sat down on the sofa, fanning herself. Peter's father, David, patted her on the back. Justice and Peter looked at each other. Justice could feel her heart beating extra fast. Was this what war was going to be like? Air raid warnings all the time, bombs dropping?

'Go and find your mask, Justice,' said Dad. 'You should leave it by the door in case you need it.'

'Will I have to take it to school?' said Justice.

'We don't know what's happening about school yet,' said Dad.

Highbury House was to remain open. Herbert rang the headmistress, Miss de Vere, the next day, and she said that everything would carry on as normal. Herbert told Justice this, adding that Highbury House would be a safe place to be.

'I don't know how you can say that,' said Justice. 'Considering it's full of murderers and kidnappers.'

She was referring to the times when she had helped solve crimes at the school. Her first two years at Highbury House seemed to have been full of dead bodies, secret tunnels and ghostly apparitions. It had been very exciting.

'Things have been fairly quiet for the last year or so,' said Herbert, with a slight smile.

'War's not exactly quiet,' said Justice. Her feelings about the coming conflict wavered between fear and a sort of horrible fascination.

'It will be for you,' said Herbert firmly.

Two weeks later Herbert drove Justice and her friend Stella to Highbury House for the new term. Stella's sister Sarah was also with them: she was about to start her second year. Sarah talked *all* the time, which Justice often found rather irritating, but today she found that she welcomed the flow of words: school, lacrosse, the exploits of her younger brothers Aaron, Gabriel and Ben, baby sister Sheila, Minky the cat, Sarah's favourite things to eat and drink . . . Justice wondered how Sarah could be related to Stella, who was always quiet but today, especially, had hardly said a word. There were seven Goldman children so maybe Sarah, who was right in the middle, had to battle to make herself heard.

'Maybe we'll have to stay in school at Christmas,' said Sarah. 'Especially if there are bombs.'

'Put a sock in it, Sarah,' said Stella.

Sarah lapsed into hurt silence that lasted until Maidstone when she piped up cheerfully: 'Will you be joining the army, Mr Jones?'

'No,' said Herbert. 'I'm far too old.'

Justice, who had held her breath, felt herself relaxing. Ever since war had been declared, she had been terrified that Dad would join up. Dad was all she had. Justice's mother, a crime writer called Veronica Burton, had died when Justice was twelve. Justice didn't think she could bear it if anything happened to her father. But Dad was forty-six; he was *definitely* too old to be a soldier.

'I'll probably carry on being a lawyer,' said Herbert. 'People will still need lawyers. I might volunteer to be an air raid warden.'

Justice's detective senses were immediately on alert. *'Always notice when people offer unnecessary detail,'* Leslie

Light, the hero of her mum's mystery novels, always said. *'It could be a sign that they have something to hide.'*

'How old do you have to be to be a soldier?' asked Sarah.

'Eighteen,' said Herbert.

'Our brother Josh is seventeen,' said Sarah.

Justice realised why Stella was being so quiet.

CHAPTER 2

It was a misty, grey afternoon. The marshes seemed to dissolve into nothingness and then, suddenly, the dark shape of Highbury House appeared on the horizon. Even Sarah stopped telling them the plot of her favourite Agatha Christie novel and stared at the apparition. As they got closer they could see the four turrets and the iron gates with stone griffins on either side. The house, never the friendliest-looking place, seemed to have a particularly dour expression that day. When they parked outside, Justice realised that this was because the windows were all covered with black curtains.

'Blackout blinds,' said Herbert. 'It's the law now.'

The blackouts were to stop lights showing and potentially guiding enemy bombers. Justice had read all about it in the papers. The dark windows were a reminder of war as was the fact that, alongside their trunks, overnight bags and hockey sticks, the girls were all carrying their gas masks.

'Seems so odd to be taking masks to school,' said Sarah.

'It's just a precaution,' said Herbert. 'I'm sure you won't have to use them.'

Stella and Sarah said thank you and goodbye to Herbert. Then they went towards the main entrance where Matron was waiting to tick them off on one of her endless lists.

Justice was left alone with her dad. He gave her a big hug. 'Goodbye, Justice. See you on the half holiday.'

'You will come, won't you?' said Justice, her voice muffled against Dad's tweed jacket.

'I promise.'

'And you won't join the army?'

'They wouldn't have me.' Dad gave Justice a kiss. 'Promise me that *you'll* be careful this term. Things will be a bit different at school.'

'I'll be OK,' said Justice. 'Nothing ever happens here.'

Dad laughed and gave Justice a final hug. 'Bye, Justice. I love you.'

'I love you too,' said Justice. Dad carried the three trunks to the porch. Hutchins, the handyman, would collect them later.

Justice didn't want to watch Dad drive away so she hurried into school, carrying her bag and hockey stick, her gas mask swinging from one hand.

'Welcome back, Justice,' said Matron. Mrs O'Brien was a rather fierce-looking woman with grey hair in a bun, but Justice knew that she was actually very kind and had a surprisingly good sense of humour.

'Hallo, Matron.'

'Have you got your health certificate? Thank you. Now, straight up to the dormy to change. Miss de Vere is going to hold a special assembly before Meal.'

This was definitely something different. The headmistress usually spoke to the students on the first morning of term, not on the first evening. Justice hurried up to the dormy, through the many doors and twisting passages. Highbury House always seemed mysteriously bigger on the inside than it was on the outside.

Justice had been in the same dormy since she had started at the school. It was called Barnowls and, although it was cramped and not particularly comfortable, it was the nearest thing to home at Highbury House. As Justice hovered outside, she could hear the girls talking – sounding more like magpies than owls – and the sound soothed her.

Justice opened the door. Stella was unpacking. Nora and Eva were chatting. Rose was brushing her hair. Letitia was reading a book. They all looked up when Justice came in.

'Justice! I've missed you.' (Letitia)

'Did you see Matron?' (Stella)

'You've got a smut on your nose. Did you know?' (Rose)

'Isn't it terrible about the war?' (Nora)

'Isn't it super?'

This last was Eva. She always thought everything was 'super', but Justice was slightly surprised that this even extended to being at war.

'What's super?' she asked, putting her bag on her bed.

'Oh, this,' said Eva vaguely, gesturing around the room that contained six beds and very little else. 'Being together. You know.'

And, despite herself, Justice did know.

The girls, now changed into their brown uniforms, clattered into the assembly hall. The blackout blinds were down and the few lights, high in the ceiling, did little to illuminate the huge room. Justice thought she could sense the nervousness all around her: the younger pupils giggling, the older ones unusually silent. She saw her friend Dorothy sitting with the sixth formers. Dorothy had once been a maid at the school but Justice's dad now paid her school fees. Dorothy was three years older than Justice but was only two years above. She'd done well in her exams and was now working for her Higher School Certificate. Dorothy gave Justice a wave and a wink.

The teachers were sitting in chairs lined up on the stage: Miss Morris the maths teacher, with whom Justice and Dorothy had shared the adventure of Smugglers' Lodge; Miss Bathurst, who taught Latin; Miss Hunting, the history teacher, who knew all the secrets of the ancient house; and Justice's favourite, Miss Heron, who taught games and would be their form mistress this year. Miss Evans, the tone-deaf music teacher, was seated at the piano which meant that shortly they would have to endure the school song. But where was Monsieur Pierre, the French teacher?

Miss de Vere seemed to appear from nowhere, striding on to the stage with her academic gown billowing behind her. She walked to the lectern and said, 'Good evening, girls.' All chattering stopped immediately. 'Welcome back to Highbury House,' she continued. 'These are challenging times but I know that you have the strength and character to endure them and to rise above them. No one would choose to live through a war but, now that war is here, we must play our part with grace and dignity. As Queen Elizabeth the

First said, "I may have the body of a weak and feeble woman but I have the heart and stomach of a king and . . . should anyone dare to invade the borders of my realm . . . I myself will take up arms."' Someone in the front row giggled and Miss de Vere glared at them before continuing, in a more business-like tone. 'I have called you together this evening because there will be some changes this term and I wanted you to know about them as soon as possible.'

Justice looked at Stella, who raised an eyebrow. What did Miss de Vere mean? Although Justice frequently complained about school, it was a constant in her life and there was something slightly frightening about the idea that it could change.

'First, I should tell you that Monsieur Pierre has returned to his native France where he has joined the army. Our thoughts go with him.' There was a slight intake of breath amongst the girls. 'Also Ada and Aggie, our housemaids, have both left to join the women's forces. I applaud them for their patriotism but this means that we will all have to pull together to do the domestic work around the school. There will be housework rotas for everyone, from first formers to the sixth.'

Justice's couldn't help smiling at the look on Rose's face. She knew that Rose would think that housework was beneath her. Justice thought it sounded much more fun than lessons.

'We will do everything we can to keep you safe here at school but there are certain precautions we must take. I know I can count on you all to be sensible about this.'

All laughter had stopped now and the faces around Justice all looked serious, even scared.

'Gas masks must be kept in a special box in each dormy. In the unlikely event of an air raid, you must collect your mask immediately. If the air raid siren sounds, students must proceed immediately to the cellars, where we have set up a comfortable shelter.'

Justice had been to the cellars before, even though they were strictly out of bounds. She couldn't imagine anywhere in the damp and dusty underground rooms being comfortable. There was a secret passage there, though. It had been boarded up for years, but maybe that was now the air raid shelter?

'Lists of form and sports captains will be posted on the notice board tomorrow,' Miss de Vere was saying. 'But I'm delighted to tell you that our new head girl is Dorothy Smith.'

There was a smattering of applause and Justice joined in enthusiastically. She was delighted for her friend. She gave Dorothy a thumbs-up and received a discreet wave back. Dorothy was blushing but she smiled as her fellow sixth-formers congratulated her. Rose's face looked stonier than ever.

'And now for my main announcement,' said Miss de Vere.

The girls sat up straighter. What could be coming now?

'As you know,' said the headmistress, 'many city schools are having to be evacuated. It is our duty to help these pupils. Therefore, as from tomorrow, we will share this building with St Wilfred's School for Boys. There will, of course, be no contact between girls and boys. The St Wilfred's boys and masters will have their own quarters and will use the playing fields at different times. Nevertheless, we must all be polite and welcoming. Now, we will sing the school song.'

CHAPTER 3

'Boys!' said Eva, for what felt like the hundredth time. 'Whatever next?'

'Boys aren't a different species, you know,' said Letitia. They were all in bed, eating a fruit cake brought by Nora from home. It was ten o'clock and lights had been turned out an hour ago. Normally Rose, as dormy captain, would be insisting that they stopped talking and went to sleep but, tonight, there was just too much to say.

'I wonder if they'll use our bathrooms.' Nora giggled.

'Miss de Vere said they'd have their own rooms,' said Stella.

'I'm sure they'll find a way of communicating with us.' With the blackout blinds down it was too dark to see Rose's face but Justice just *knew* that she was tossing back her hair and smiling complacently. Rose was always talking about the many boys who were in love with her. They all had names like Algernon or Binky and, from the photos Rose kept in her diary, looked pale and spotty. But they sent love letters, while on Valentine's Day last year, Rose had received seven cards. For this reason alone, she was much admired by the younger girls.

'I'm sure all the St Wilfred's boys will fall madly in love with you, Rose,' said Letitia.

Justice knew from Letitia's voice that she was teasing but Eva, as usual, took it literally.

'Rose is *so* beautiful. *Of course* they'll be in love with her.'

'Stop,' said Rose. Meaning *Go on*.

'I hope there will be some mysteries to solve this year,' said Justice. 'Maybe one of the St Wilfred's masters will be a German spy.'

'Do grow up,' said Rose. 'We're at war. Isn't that enough for you?'

Justice felt rather squashed. Rose was right. War was serious. She shouldn't be thinking about mysteries at a time like this. All the same, she was excited at the thought of new people coming into the school. She knew everyone at Highbury House and felt that she'd solved every mystery the place had to offer. Maybe St Wilfred's would include some interesting characters – as well as hundreds of boys dying of love for Rose.

'Think of the tricks we can play on them,' said Letitia. She was the form's champion prankster, whether it was hiding in a cupboard during music lessons and playing discordant notes on her recorder, or dressing up as a chimney sweep to fool Mrs Hopkirk, the housekeeper. Letitia just didn't care about school rules and, while this made her a lot of fun, Justice did find her friend rather exhausting at times. Stella was a much more restful companion.

Tonight Stella was quieter than ever. Justice was sure that she was thinking about Josh. In six months' time, Josh would have to join the army. She prayed the war would be over by then.

'I'm more concerned about having to do housework,' said Rose. 'What a cheek. My parents don't pay school fees for me to clean the floors. I'll get the pater to complain.'

'The pater' was Rose's important diplomat father. Justice wondered what Mr Trevellian-Hayes thought about the war. Rose had once said that he admired Adolf Hitler, though that was before anyone knew very much about him.

'Someone has to do the housework,' said Nora.

'It's maids' work,' said Rose. 'Surely Miss de Vere could get maids from somewhere.'

'Everyone's doing war work now,' said Letitia. 'My mother says that, after the war, there won't be any servants.'

'Don't be ridiculous,' said Rose. 'There will always be servants. Talking of maids, what do you think about your little friend being head girl, Justice?'

'I think Dorothy will be a brilliant head girl,' said Justice. It had taken Rose a lot of time to get used to the former maid becoming a pupil and she clearly still didn't think that Dorothy deserved to be at Highbury House. She always called her 'your little friend', although Dorothy was now rather tall and elegant. *Keep your temper*, Justice told herself. She didn't want a row with Rose on their first night back.

'Dorothy's so clever,' said Eva. 'I don't think I'll ever pass my School Certificate.'

As everyone secretly agreed with this, there was a sudden flurry to change the subject.

The next day, there was a plan of the school on the notice board, some areas shaded in red. The St Wilfred's boys were to have their meals, and most of their lessons, in the assembly hall. They would have their dormitories on the first floor and would use the main staircase to move between the two. The girls would use the maids' staircase by the kitchen, and would keep their dormies on the second floor.

'Typical,' said Rose. 'It's like we really are maids now. Wait till I tell the pater.'

'The lists of form captains is up,' said Stella. The girls crowded round. Moira Campbell, Justice's friend from the cross-country team, was the fifth-form captain. Who was sports captain? Surely not . . .

'Justice Jones, *sports captain?*' said Rose. 'Is this a joke?'

Justice thought the same. The captains changed every term so, in theory, everyone got a turn, but Justice knew that she was the worst in the class at sport. She'd never mastered lacrosse and now was allowed to miss practice and read a book in the library instead.

'Justice is brilliant at cross-country running,' said Stella. Strangely enough, this was true. Running never seemed like a game to Justice. There was no catching or throwing required; it was just about keeping going. And, if the last few years had taught Justice anything, it was to keep going.

'Congratulations, Justice,' said Nora. 'I wonder if we'll have to do games with the boys.'

This was a thought. The girls discussed it all through breakfast, where it was very strange to see Dorothy stand up and say grace. '*Benedictus benedicat,*' said the new head girl, with admirable composure. It was even stranger to see the first years, who were on 'pantry duty', collecting the dirty plates and carrying them into the scullery to wash up. The fifth years were on 'dusting and polishing' that week. Justice couldn't wait.

As the girls clattered off to their first lessons, Justice stayed behind to tie up her shoelace. She hoped she might get a chance to talk to Dorothy but the sixth formers stayed in the refectory, deep in conversation.

Justice did see something else, though: a bus drawing up outside the main entrance.

The St Wilfred's boys had arrived.

CHAPTER 4

Quick as a flash, Justice darted behind one of the suits of armour in the great hall. The last three years had taught her how to disappear at will. The school was full of hidden alcoves and secret cupboards where you could hide from a passing teacher. There were also lots of monstrous pieces of furniture you could duck behind. The great hall was full of such things: suits of armour, a grandfather clock, two trophy cabinets and a vast bookcase. There were also long velvet curtains covering the many arched windows.

From her vantage point, Justice watched the boys troop into the hall. They were wearing red blazers, grey jumpers and grey shorts. There seemed to be a great many of them but, trying to speed-count, Justice only got to fifty. There were over one hundred girls at Highbury House. Was St

Wilfred's a smaller school, or had some of the boys stayed behind in London? The pupils seemed to range from smallish boys, who looked about ten, to lanky creatures who were probably Justice's own age of fifteen.

There were two masters with them: one a youngish man with sandy hair; the other older with a bristly moustache and the swaggering walk of someone used to being in command.

'Line up, boys,' yelled Moustache. 'Silence!' All chatter stopped. Justice saw the boys looking at each other. *They obey the teacher,* she thought, *but they don't like him.*

'Major Hammond.' Miss de Vere swept down the stairs. Justice prayed that the headmistress wouldn't look too closely at the nearest suit of armour because, of course, Miss de Vere knew the school's hiding places too.

'Welcome to Highbury House,' said Miss de Vere, at her most regal.

'Thank you for taking us in.' Major Hammond made a slight bow. He was obviously already under the headmistress's spell. 'This is my colleague, Mr Hoffman, and these are the waifs and strays.' He waved a hand at the red blazers.

'Welcome, all of you,' said Miss de Vere. She was standing on the bottom step and Justice could no longer see her face, but she guessed that the headmistress was smiling at the boys because a few of them smiled back. They all looked slightly surprised. Justice betted that Major Hammond didn't smile at them often.

'If you make your way into the assembly hall through the double doors on the left,' said Miss de Vere, 'I will explain the arrangements we have made for you. I hope you'll all be very happy here.'

'Door on the left,' yelled Major Hammond. 'Quick, march!'

The boys marched and, in a few seconds, the hall was empty. Apart from Miss de Vere, who said, without looking round, 'Go back to class, Justice.'

There was no chance to talk in the Latin class but, in recess, Justice told the Barnowls all about her glimpse of the St Wilfred's contingent.

'The older man, Major Hammond, looked like he might be strict. He's probably the headmaster. The other teacher, Mr Hoffman, was younger.'

'I wonder why he's not in uniform,' said Rose. 'I hope he's not a conchie. I hate conchies.'

Justice knew that 'conchie' was an insulting word used to describe 'conscientious objectors' – people who felt that it was wrong to fight in a war. Conscientious objectors were often called cowards but Justice thought that it was rather brave to stand up for your principles in this way. She didn't say this to Rose, though.

'Were there really only fifty of them?' said Stella.

'I counted about fifty,' said Justice. 'Maybe they only brought the ones who didn't have anywhere else to go. Major Hammond called them "waifs and strays".'

'He sounds a real charmer,' said Nora, pulling a face.

'Never mind the teachers,' said Rose. 'What are the boys like? Especially the older ones.'

They didn't see the boys all morning. At lunchtime the girls heard voices and clattering cutlery in the assembly hall but, much to their disappointment, no one emerged. After lunch, the fifth formers started their domestic duties. They were given dusters and brooms and told to sweep the corridors. Justice and Stella were allotted the first floor. Much to their mutual annoyance, Rose was put with them.

'This is such a cheek,' said Rose, flicking her feather duster over a gloomy oil painting of a past headmistress. 'I've written to my pater. He'll tell Miss de Vere that I can't be made to do housework.'

Justice wasn't sure about that. She thought Miss de Vere would be a match even for Rose's Important Diplomat father.

'The first floor's quite interesting though,' said Justice. 'We might be able to hear Miss de Vere talking in her study.'

'Or see the boys,' said Stella, with a sly look at Rose. 'Their dormies are here, and I think they have some lessons here too.'

Miss de Vere's study was in the South Turret. It was reached by a spiral staircase from the first floor. The corridor beyond that had a notice saying 'St Wilfred's boys only'.

'Why aren't the boys doing chores too?' said Justice. 'That's what I want to know.'

'Boys don't do *housework*,' said Rose, sounding shocked.

'Why not?' said Justice. 'Anyway, as we're here, let's take advantage of it. We're maids. Maids can go anywhere.'

She set off along the corridor, pushing her broom in front of her like an alibi. Most of the rooms had been turned into dormitories, some with as many as ten beds in them. The last door was shut and Justice could hear voices inside.

'Let's go.' Stella grabbed her arm.

'If we get into trouble,' said Rose, 'I'll say it was all your idea.'

But Justice couldn't help herself. She crept closer. The voices seemed to be in a foreign language. Was it a French lesson? But Monsieur Pierre had left the school. Then, to her surprise, music started playing. She knew it couldn't be

Miss Evans and the school orchestra. It was in tune, for one thing. Justice gently turned the handle and pushed the door open with her broom.

The room was empty apart from a wireless playing on its own.

After Meal, the cross-country team – Justice, Stella, Letitia, Rose, Alicia and Moira – went out for a run with Miss Heron.

Justice always enjoyed these evening runs. It felt as if they were escaping from school, while the action of running – her feet pounding on road or grass – made her forget her worries for a while. They followed Miss Heron through the school gates and took the path across the marshes. They usually did the same circuit, running as far as the crossroads that led to the village and then back to school and around the top field. As Justice kept pace with Stella, the long grass on either side of them almost shoulder-high in places, she found that she wasn't thinking about school, Dad or even the war. She was just a running machine: heart, muscle and sinew. It was getting darker and she could smell the sea. She wished she could keep running for ever.

It wasn't until they jogged back through the school gates that reality returned. Rose, who was in front, stopped suddenly.

'Keep going,' said Miss Heron, who was now at the back.

Rose pointed. The playing field was full of figures in red tops, chasing a ball around, regardless of the fact that it was almost dark.

'It's only the St Wilfred's boys playing football,' said Miss Heron. 'Keep moving, girls.'

Justice felt very self-conscious, running along the edge of the lacrosse pitch. Or was it a football pitch now? She thought the game looked quite fun, a lot easier than lacrosse anyhow. How hard could it be to kick a ball? As she watched, a fair-haired boy took a swing at the ball and missed completely.

'Anderson!' groaned the other boys. There was something in their voices that made Justice think that Anderson missed the ball a lot. She felt a stab of fellow feeling.

By now, the boys had noticed them and stopped playing. There were a few whistles and someone called, 'Hallo, blondie!'

'Stop that!' shouted Mr Hoffman, trotting up, wearing cricket flannels and looking out of breath. The boys ignored him.

'Quiet!' shouted Miss Heron. The whistling stopped immediately. 'Carry on with your game,' she said to the nearest boys, 'and try to behave like gentlemen.'

'Thank you,' panted Mr Hoffman.

Miss Heron nodded to him. 'Keep going, girls,' she said again. Rose and Alicia had stopped at the other end of the pitch and appeared to be chatting to two of the boys.

It didn't surprise Justice to learn, in the dormy later, that Rose had a new admirer.

CHAPTER 5

Rose's new friend was called Carrington. 'All the boys are called by their surnames,' Rose informed the Barnowls. Justice remembered the cries of 'Anderson!' when the fair-haired boy missed the ball. It must be awful never to be called by your first name, even when people were annoyed with you.

'He's fifteen,' said Rose. 'He wants to meet me in the grounds after lights out one evening.'

'You got through a lot in the three minutes you spoke to him,' said Justice.

'He said meeting me was like being struck by lightning,' said Rose, tossing her golden hair, which was loose for the night.

Rose was being so annoying Justice almost wished she

would be struck by lightning, but she didn't want an argument. Dormy time was different now. They had to make sure the blackout blinds were down before Matron did her rounds. Then Hutchins patrolled from the outside and any dormy that was 'showing a light' got an order mark. Miss Morris was an air raid warden and she was very strict about sticking to the rules. There were typewritten instructions pinned on the door:

<u>In case of an air raid</u>
Put on dressing gown and slippers and proceed
    immediately to the cellars
Bring your gas mask
Do not bring any personal items
Do not run
Do not talk

It was pitch-black when the lights were turned off. Justice could no longer see the moon from her bed.

'Just think of Carrington and his friends sleeping right below us,' said Rose with a giggle.

'I'm sure he can't sleep because he's thinking of you,' said Justice.

'It's so romantic,' said Eva.

'Carrington-io and Juliet,' put in Nora.

Everyone laughed, except Rose, who told them all to be quiet.

Under the covers, Justice got out her journal and torch.

Highbury House at war, she wrote.

<u>Things that are different</u>
Blackout blinds
Gas masks
Boys

<u>Things that are the same</u>
Awful food
Cross country
Rose

'Justice!' hissed Rose. 'I can see your torch. Turn it off.'

'It's hardly enough light to guide Hitler to drop a bomb on us,' said Justice.

'Don't,' whimpered Eva.

Eva's right for once, thought Justice, turning off her torch. It really wasn't something to make a joke about.

*   *   *

At breakfast, Justice received two messages. One more welcome than the other. The first was a note from Dorothy.

Can you come up to my room after prep? There might be a new mystery!

Justice smiled. Dorothy knew how much she loved a mystery. Justice looked over to the prefects' table and nodded her head. Dorothy winked at her.

The second message told her to report to Miss de Vere before first lesson.

What have I done now? thought Justice, as she climbed the spiral staircase to Miss de Vere's study. She didn't *think* she'd broken any school rules but she couldn't be sure. Maybe Miss de Vere wanted to tell her off for hiding behind the suit of armour yesterday. *It couldn't be about Dad, could it?* Justice found her heart pounding as she knocked on the door.

But the headmistress seemed to be in a good mood. 'Good morning, Justice. Are you enjoying being back at school?'

'Yes, Miss de Vere.' This was always the right answer.

'I know that things are different this term but we're still the same school family.'

'Yes, Miss de Vere.'

'I hope that you'll work hard for your School Certificate. You have the potential to do really well. Both your father and I think so. You could go on to take Highers. Maybe even go to university.'

'Yes, Miss de Vere.' Justice's mother had studied classics at Cambridge but hadn't been allowed to take a degree because she was a woman. Things were different now, Justice knew, but what if the war went on for years? Did people go to university in wartime?

'I noticed that you were curious about the St Wilfred's boys.'

This time Justice said nothing.

'As you know, I had initially thought that there would be no contact between the two schools but I have come to think that some cooperation might be mutually beneficial. Perhaps we can have a civilising effect.' She smiled to show this was a joke.

Justice wondered if the headmistress had heard about the boys wolf-whistling at the cross-country team. That certainly hadn't felt very civilised.

'I'd like the fifth-form sports captains to work together to plan some sort of joint event,' said Miss de Vere. 'There are no sixth formers at St Wilfred's. Therefore, you will meet the St Wilfred's sports captain in here after prep tonight. His name' – Miss de Vere consulted a list – 'is Henry Anderson. I will leave you alone together but you must only discuss the matter in hand. Is that clear?'

'Yes, Miss de Vere.'

Justice was going to have a busy evening.

CHAPTER 6

Henry Anderson stood up when Justice entered the room.

'Sit down, Henry,' said Miss de Vere. 'There's no need to stand on ceremony with Justice.'

'I once knew someone with a cat called Ceremony,' said Justice. 'It was so that they could say "Don't stand on Ceremony." Meaning the cat . . .' Her voice died away. Miss de Vere raised an eyebrow. Henry Anderson just stared. He had thick glasses on, which made his blue eyes look very big. He hadn't been wearing them playing football, which was probably why he missed the ball.

'I'll leave you two to discuss sports fixtures,' said Miss de Vere. 'I'll be downstairs in the staff room.' She managed to make this sound vaguely like a threat. She also left the door slightly open.

Left alone, Justice and Henry looked at each other. They were sitting side by side. Justice suddenly got up and went to sit on the other side of the desk. In Miss de Vere's chair.

'I say,' said Henry. 'Are you allowed to do that?'

Justice shrugged. 'Probably not. I just wanted to see what it felt like. I did it once before. Mind you, Miss de Vere caught me then.'

'If old Hammy caught one of us sitting in his chair, I think he'd kill us.'

'Is that Major Hammond? I thought he seemed strict. I was in the great hall when you first arrived.'

'I didn't see you.'

'I was hiding behind a suit of armour.'

Henry laughed suddenly, making him look much younger. 'Are all the girls here like you?'

'What do you mean?'

'Not caring about the rules and all that.'

'No,' said Justice regretfully. 'Most of them like the rules. Except my friend Letitia, that is.'

'Is she the blonde girl who was running with you?'

'No, that was Rose.'

'Rose. She looked . . .'

'Beautiful? Stunning? Gorgeous?'

'Stuck-up, I thought. Carrington liked her, though. And if Carrington liked her, everyone else has to. He's that sort.'

'Rose is that sort too.'

They smiled at each other. Somehow, they seemed to have skipped the beginning part of getting to know each other and had become friends.

Half-seriously, Justice held out her hand across Miss de Vere's desk. 'My name's Justice. Justice Jones.'

'Anderson.' They shook hands.

'Your name's really Henry, though, isn't it?'

'Yes, but we only use surnames at school. If anyone hears your first name, they rag you for weeks.'

'Sounds horrible.'

'You get used to it.'

'How long have you been at St Wilfred's?'

'Since I was thirteen. I was a day boy until the war came so it wasn't that bad.'

'I've been at Highbury House since I was twelve. I'd never been to school before. It felt like I was living in a nightmare. Or a gothic horror novel. Well, there *was* a murder here in my first term.'

'*What?*' Henry eyes were huge behind his glasses.

'I'll tell you all about it another time. I suppose we should talk about this sports thing. Miss de Vere is sure to come back soon.' Plus, Justice wanted to visit Dorothy before bedtime.

Henry seemed to slump in his chair. 'I don't know what to say. I hate sport.'

'So do I,' said Justice.

'But you were out running yesterday.'

'That's cross-country. It's different. I can't do any sport that involves throwing or catching. You should see me playing lacrosse. Well, I don't even try any more. I read in the library instead.'

'Lucky you,' said Henry. 'I have to play football and rugby and I loathe them. Cricket too.'

'Why are you sports captain then?'

'Mr Hoffman decided. He just picked the first name on the list. I'm at the top. A for Anderson.'

'What's Mr Hoffman like? I saw him when you all arrived.'

'He's new this term. He seems all right. The other boys rag him, though.'

Justice remembered how the boys had ignored their teacher yesterday. She was beginning to think that 'ragging' was nastier than it sounded.

'Why don't we suggest a rounders match?' said Justice. 'Mixed teams. That's not a bad game, really. If you're fielding you can think about other things.'

'And you can see the trees and the birds,' said Henry. 'I like birdwatching.'

Justice could just imagine what Carrington and co would say about this hobby.

'That's settled then,' said Justice. 'Good work, Henry.'

Henry laughed. 'It feels strange to hear someone call me Henry. Tell you what, you call me Henry and I'll call you Jones.'

Justice quite liked the sound of that.

Luckily, Justice had returned to the other side of the desk before the headmistress came back into the room. Miss de Vere approved the idea of a rounders match. She seemed pleased that Justice and Henry had been able to come to an agreement. Miss de Vere chatted graciously to them for a few minutes and Justice learnt that Henry lived in Weybridge and was an only child. Like Justice. Henry said that he liked reading and Miss de Vere, who was an author herself, told him that Justice's mother had written detective stories. 'I say,' said Henry. 'That's wonderful.' Justice had smiled but she hadn't wanted to talk about her mum because there was always a moment when she had to say 'she was' and acknowledge, all over again, that her mother was dead.

The dormitory bell was ringing when they left Miss de Vere's study.

'I'd better hurry,' said Henry. 'Old Hammy goes mad if we're late.' He darted off along the corridor. Justice took the main stairs up to the second floor where the dormitories were. She would get an order mark for being late but, unlike Henry, it didn't really bother her.

Dorothy, as head girl, now had her own room. Justice thought it was very cosy, with the desk lamp glowing, picking out the colours in Dorothy's patchwork quilt. Justice remembered that quilt from the days when Dorothy had slept in the maids' room in the attics. She still had her teddy bear too.

They sat on the bed and exchanged news. They knew each other's families well and Dorothy often stayed with Justice in the holidays.

'I'm so glad Dad works on a farm,' said Dorothy. 'That means he won't have to join the army. Farming's a reserved occupation.'

'I'm glad my dad's too old,' said Justice.

'John keeps saying he wants to join up when he's eighteen,' said Dorothy. Dorothy's younger brother was fifteen. He worked on the farm with his father.

'Surely the war will be over by then,' said Justice.

'I hope so,' said Dorothy. 'If it's still going on after Highers I think I'll be a Land Girl. You know, help out on a farm.'

Justice had seen posters for the Land Army: women ploughing fields at sunset, lit by the rays of the setting sun. She had a feeling that the reality would be very different.

'Won't you go to university?' she asked, remembering Miss de Vere's words yesterday.

'I'd like to,' said Dorothy. 'I'd have to get a scholarship, though. I can't ask your dad to pay any more fees. But I'll wait until the war is over. It's strange, isn't it? Everyone keeps talking about the war but nothing seems to be happening.'

The newspapers were calling it the 'phony war'. When the sirens had gone off as soon as war was declared, Justice had thought that that was what it was going to be like from then on: sirens, bombs, constant terror. But, since that day, the sirens had been silent. Justice knew, of course, that terrible things were happening in Europe: Poland was occupied; Jewish people were being treated appallingly, not allowed to live and work freely, and forced to wear yellow stars for identification. Some Jewish children had been able to escape to England and Justice had seen pictures of them on the news, arriving at Liverpool Street Station, looking so vulnerable, clutching their small pieces of luggage – all that was left of their old life. But, at Highbury House, the war had just become another thing to complain about.

'Dad says it won't stay this way for long,' said Justice.

'He's probably right,' said Dorothy. 'He knows things, your dad.'

There was a brief silence and then Justice said, 'So what's this mystery then?'

'Well,' said Dorothy, tucking her legs under herself and getting comfortable. 'You know the sixth-form common room is in the attic?'

'Of course.' Justice had a map of the school with all the rooms marked, including secret doors and hidden passageways.

'Well, I went up there last night after lights out. I'd left my book in the common room. It was really dark with all the blackouts up but I found the book and I was creeping back when I heard voices coming from the North Turret.'

'Really?' The turret room was kept locked but Dorothy and Justice had heard voices coming from there before. Once it had been Miss de Vere using a radio to call for help. Now, there was a telephone installed in the North Turret, one of only two in the school.

'Who could it have been?' asked Justice.

'One of the St Wilfred's teachers, Mr Hoffman, is sleeping up in the attic. He's got my old room.'

'I can't imagine a teacher sleeping there.'

'Nor can I. It's been empty ever since I stopped being a maid, because Ada and Aggie didn't live in. Major Hammond's been given Monsieur Pierre's room.'

'I miss Monsieur Pierre. I didn't think I would.'

'So do I. He gave me a book when he left. He knew I was doing French for my Highers.' She showed Justice a book with a top hat on the cover. *Arsène Lupin, Gentleman-cambrioleur* by Maurice Leblanc.

'It means "gentleman thief",' said Dorothy. 'Monsieur Pierre said he knew I liked mysteries.'

Thinking of French made Justice remember the wireless playing in the empty room yesterday. She had been sure that the voices were speaking in a foreign language. She told Dorothy, who was mystified.

'I don't think there's a spare wireless in the school. There's one in every common room and I think Matron has one in sick bay. St Wilfred's must have brought their own. But why leave it playing on its own?'

'I don't know. It's another mystery. Do you think it was Mr Hoffman on the phone last night?'

45

'I'm not sure,' said Dorothy, 'but I think it's suspicious that someone was on the phone in the dead of night.'

Justice had to stifle a smile. 'The dead of night' was one of Dorothy's favourite phrases. 'We ought to watch Mr Hoffman closely,' she said. 'I've made friends with one of the boys. Henry Anderson. Maybe he can help.'

'Do you trust him?'

'Yes,' said Justice. 'I think I do. I'd better go now. I'm awfully late for dormy.'

'Say I kept you,' said Dorothy. 'That might work.'

Justice grinned. 'I keep forgetting how important you are now,' she said.

CHAPTER 7

Dearest Dad,

It seems strange that THE BOYS have only been here for
two weeks. I'm putting them in capitals because that's how
the girls here talk about them. THE BOYS have their own
quarters and we're not meant to mix but Rose, of course,
already has an admirer. I've been asked to set up a sports
event for both schools. Can you believe I'm sports captain,
Dad? I can't. Anyway, I've had to organise it with the
St Wilfred sports captain. He's called Henry and he hates
games even more than I do!

    Did you know Dorothy was head girl? I was so happy
when Miss DV told us. Dorothy is now the school idol,

just like Helena Bliss used to be. Did you know Helena is married now? Rose showed me the pictures in one of her society magazines. Helena was in yards of white lace and she looked very pleased with herself. She's married a lord so that's probably why.

Everything at school is the same and yet it's different. That's partly because of THE BOYS and partly because of the war. Because nothing is happening here (I know it is in other places) it's hard to believe that there really is a war on. We had an air raid practice the other day and it was a disaster! It was very dark and some girls fell downstairs. Eva got lost. The shelter is in the cellars, in those underground rooms. It was very crowded when we were all down there and it smelt musty. Rose saw a rat and had hysterics. The tunnel is still boarded up. Yes, I had a look but I didn't go near it. I promise!

One thing that's different is that we're doing housework now. I really like it because you get a chance to see all the bits of the school that are usually out of bounds. Rose's father wrote to complain but Dorothy says Miss DV wrote back saying that nobody was above domestic work. Dorothy seems to know everything now she's head girl.

What's it like being an air raid warden? Do you have to go round yelling at people if there's a gap in their blackout? Hutchins shouts 'Showing a light!' if there's just the tiniest chink in our curtains and the whole dormy gets an order mark. Still, I'm glad you've got a nice SAFE war job. Make sure you do go into the shelter if there IS an air raid. Can't wait to see you on the half holiday. Can you send a tuck box? I know it's difficult with food shortages but Miss Lewis has probably got black market contacts (JOKE).

The 'mixed' rounders match is tomorrow. Wish me luck.

Lots of love,
Justice

Justice folded the letter and put it into its envelope. A previous matron had insisted on reading their letters home so they had to leave them unsealed. Mrs O'Brien would never do such a thing but, even so, Justice hadn't told her dad the really secret things, like the mystery of the voices in the turret room. That would have to wait until she saw him on the half holiday in October.

They were in prep. This was the time in the evening when they were meant to do homework, write letters home or practise instruments. Most of the girls had their heads in their textbooks. With the School Certificate exams coming up, the teachers were suddenly piling on the work. Rose was reading a magazine tucked inside a history book and Eva was drawing a picture. She was good at art and Justice tried to sneak a look but, unusually, Eva put up an arm to protect her work.

Justice went up to Camilla, the prefect who was meant to be in charge. 'I've got a meeting with Henry Anderson. About tomorrow's rounders match. Can I go?'

'OK,' said Camilla, looking at her rather curiously. 'Just put your letter in the pile there and don't be late for dormy.'

Henry was in Miss de Vere's sitting room. This was a little room off the main entrance where Miss de Vere interviewed prospective parents. Because of this, it was full of trophies and other subtle boasts. There were twenty-three trophies to be exact. Justice knew because she had polished them last week. She also knew that, with the exception of the cross-country cup she and her friends had won two years ago, all the rest dated back to the 1920s. She was almost missing dusting and polishing. The fifth years were on pantry duty this week. Washing up for two hundred people was an exhausting task. It was only Wednesday and already Justice's hands were red raw.

'I thought you were never coming,' said Henry. He looked rather downcast, shoulders hunched in his red blazer.

'I had to finish a letter to my dad,' said Justice.

'I never know what to say to my parents,' said Henry. 'My father only wants to know about games – how I scored the winning goal and all that. As if!'

'Well, you can write to him about the rounders match,' said Justice.

Henry groaned. 'It's going to be a disaster.'

'Of course it isn't,' said Justice. She knew by now that you had to ignore Henry's occasional fits of gloom. He was a cheerful companion most of the time but talking about games, Major Hammond or his father always made him depressed.

'Let's look at the team lists again,' said Justice.

Henry took two rather crumpled pieces of paper out of his pocket. Henry and Justice had made themselves team captains, if only because they knew it would annoy Carrington and Rose.

'Carrington will keep yelling at me to "play up",' said Henry.

'Do what I do to Rose,' said Justice. 'I keep telling her how brilliantly she's playing. She never knows if I'm joking or not but she can hardly argue with it. '

'I'd never dare do that with Carrington,' said Henry.

Justice sighed. She sympathised with Henry but his mood was starting to affect hers. 'It'll be fine,' she said. 'You'll see.'

'I hope it rains tomorrow,' said Henry.

They made a few changes to the teams and played a game or two of noughts and crosses. Then the dormitory bell went. They could hear the boys charging up the main stairs; the girls, of course, were still using the maids' staircase at the back of the house.

'I'd better go,' said Henry.

'We needn't hurry,' said Justice. 'They know we're arranging the match. Tell you what, let's do some exploring. Do you want to see the North Turret? My friend Dorothy heard sinister voices there last week.'

Henry laughed. 'Jones, you'll get us both expelled.' But he didn't say no.

The first-floor corridor was deserted although they could hear voices coming from the boys' dormitories. The second floor, too, was empty. Justice led the way to the attic stairs.

'We have to be quiet. Mr Hoffman's room is up here.'

'Oh, he'll be supervising dormitories,' said Henry. 'Or trying to.'

All the doors in the attic corridor were shut. Justice knew them by heart: Dorothy's old room, the sixth-form common room, the art studio – unused now, after Mr Davenport's departure. The last door led into the North Turret. Out of habit, Justice tried the handle, fully expecting it to be locked. The door opened.

'Let's go in,' she said.

'We can't,' said Henry. But he was right behind her.

The round room was empty apart from a desk with a telephone on it. But what made Justice gasp was the face at the window.

A window three storeys high.

CHAPTER 8

As Justice and Henry stood there, staring, the face suddenly disappeared from view. Had the person fallen? Justice ran to the narrow window and looked down. It was too dark to see anything outside but she couldn't hear any blood-curdling screams.

'Is there anything there?' said Henry. 'Anyone, I mean?'

'Not that I can see,' said Justice. She turned to look at Henry realising, as she did so, that there were no blackout blinds in this room. It was amazing how much you could see without them, even at night time. Henry's face looked pale in the cloudy moonlight.

'He was there, wasn't he?' said Henry. 'The man. I didn't just imagine him?'

'I don't even know if it was a man,' said Justice. 'But there was someone there.'

'It was a man,' said Henry. 'But I didn't recognise him. And I'm good at remembering faces.'

'But how did he get there?' said Justice. 'We're on the third floor here.'

'Is there a ledge or something?' said Henry. He went to the window and opened it. Justice was rather impressed by this. Instead of running away or calling a teacher, her new friend was investigating. Perhaps Henry, too, was a secret detective.

'There's a narrow ledge,' said Henry. 'He could have balanced on it. But why? And where is he now?'

Justice looked out. The grounds were dark and deserted. In a few minutes, Hutchins would start patrolling the grounds, checking that the blackout was secure. She shut the window hastily.

'We'd better go, but we need to discuss this.'

'Should we tell someone?' said Henry.

'Not yet,' said Justice. 'Let's investigate by ourselves first.'

'OK,' said Henry. 'You're the boss, Jones.'

No one had ever said that to Justice before. She liked it.

*   *   *

Justice got back to her dormy before Matron made her rounds.

'You're late,' said Rose, who was already in bed. She always managed to use the bathroom first.

'Sorry,' said Justice. She thought she'd better apologise because Rose was still dormy captain. 'I was just talking to Henry about the rounders match. Last-minute arrangements.'

'Honestly,' said Rose, 'anyone would think you were in love with Henry.' She laughed to show this was a joke.

'Don't be stupid,' snapped Eva. 'Justice isn't in love with Henry.'

They all stared. Eva was never angry with anyone and she was certainly *never* cross with Rose, whom she worshipped. Justice and Stella exchanged glances. Rose's mouth was open in surprise. Eva's face was flushed but she carried on getting ready for bed. Letitia looked as if she was going to laugh and then thought better of it. Not even Nora could think of anything to say.

It was only the arrival of Matron that broke the spell. 'Get a move on, girls. Justice, you haven't even started getting ready. Ten minutes before lights out.'

Justice hurried into the freezing bathroom, had a quick wash and then changed into her pyjamas. The Barnowls were all silent when she returned. Letitia and Nora were reading. Rose and Eva were pretending to be asleep.

Justice got into bed and exchanged another mystified look with Stella. She'd been looking forward to telling her about the face at the window but she could tell there would be no chatting tonight.

'Night, all,' said Justice.

'Night,' chorused Letitia, Stella and Nora.

Rose and Eva stayed silent.

Justice wrote in her journal.

Mysteries to investigate
1. *Mysterious voices in the North Turret*
2. *The face at the window*
3. *The wireless playing on its own*

Other strange things
1. *Why is Eva suddenly so angry?*
2. *Why did M. Pierre give Dorothy a book about a thief?*
3. *Why is Rose so annoying?*

She knew the answer to the last one, but it made her feel better to write it down.

CHAPTER 9

Henry's wish was not granted. The next day was bright and sunny, perfect weather for the rounders match.

The Barnowls still seemed subdued after last night but Rose took the time to tell Justice that the event would be a disaster. 'I just hope you've got some good players on your team,' she said, twisting her hair into the high ponytail that she had made the school fashion.

'Well, you're on Henry's team,' said Justice. They had decided this last night. Carrington was on Justice's.

'Whose team am I on?' asked Letitia.

'Mine,' said Justice. 'I'm going to pin the lists up on the notice board but you can look now, if you want. My team is called the Lightning Bolts.' She'd chosen the name because the detective in Mum's books had been called Leslie Light. Henry's team was called the Defenders.

'I'm a Defender,' said Eva, looking at the sheet.

'So am I,' said Nora.

Stella was on Justice's team. She hoped it didn't look like favouritism. She'd suggested that Henry put his best friend in his team but he'd said that he didn't have one.

'It'll be super,' said Eva.

Justice was glad that she'd regained her good spirits.

After lunch, they all trooped out onto the top field. There were fifteen people on each team so all the fifth years from both schools were included.

The Lightning Bolts
1. *Justice Jones (captain)*
2. *Stella Goldman*
3. *Letitia Blackstock*
4. *Moira Campbell*
5. *Joan Kirby*
6. *Susan Smythe*
7. *Flora McDonald*
8. *Elizabeth Moore*

9. Jonathan Carrington
10. Humphrey Fellows
11. Justin French
12. Alastair Monkton-Price
13. Percy Malone
14. Wilfred Yardley
15. Roger Green

The Defenders

1. Henry Anderson (captain)
2. Rose Trevellian-Hayes
3. Alicia Butterfield
4. Cecilia Delaney
5. Eva Harris-Brown
6. Nora Wilkinson
7. Freda Saxe-Johnson
8. Irene Atkins
9. Salim Khan
10. Steven Meek
11. Godfrey George
12. Frederick Blake
13. Daniel Jacobson
14. Nicholas Francis
15. Leonard Hastings

Miss Heron and Mr Hoffman were refereeing the match but Justice was sure that the Highbury House teacher would have the last word. Miss Heron looked very efficient in her cricket jumper and divided skirts. Mr Hoffman was just wearing an ordinary shirt and trousers, though he had rolled his sleeves up and taken off his tie.

They tossed a coin to see who would bat first.

'Heads,' said Justice.

'Tails,' said Henry.

The sixpence glittered in the sun before coming to rest on the grass, the king's head upwards.

The Lightning Bolts were to bat first. The field was marked out with four posts. The idea was for the batter to hit the ball hard enough to give them time to run around the posts. The fielders' job was to catch the ball and throw it to one of the posts. If it was caught at the post before the runner reached it, that player was out. If you couldn't get all the way round on your hit, it was still considered good to get to the second or third post and score half a rounder.

'Good luck,' said Justice to Henry.

'And you.' Henry squared his shoulders as he went to organise his fielders. At Justice's suggestion he was wearing his glasses, so at least he'd be able to see them.

Justice decided to bat first. That way, if she missed

completely, at least it would be over quickly. She put Carrington last, as he was meant to be so good at sport. Moira, who'd once hit the ball so hard it broke a greenhouse window, was before him.

'I hope you know what you're doing,' said Carrington, as Justice picked up the bat.

'Of course I do.' Justice gave him a big smile. She was sure that Rose would have told Carrington about Justice's inability to hit, throw or catch.

A boy called Meek who, according to Henry's description, wasn't particularly, was going to bowl. Miss Heron called Justice forward and blew her whistle to start the game.

Meek threw the ball. Justice swung her bat and, to her utter surprise, made contact.

'Run, Justice!' yelled her team.

The ball hadn't gone far but it got Justice to the first post. Did she dare to try for the second? She did.

'Stay there!' someone (probably Carrington) shouted. Justice stayed.

'Half a rounder,' shouted Miss Heron.

'Well done, Justice,' called Stella, as she came to take her place at the batting square.

Stella hit the ball well and started running. Justice ran too and reached home to score their first full rounder. Stella ran all the way round to make it two. The girls grinned at each other.

'Well played!' shouted Henry from the top of the field, where he was probably birdwatching.

The next few players missed the ball completely but the following Lightning Bolts managed to amass another four rounders. Then it was Moira's turn. She took an almighty swing and the ball flew over the fielders' heads, disappearing into the trees.

Moira jogged around the circle. 'Can I go again?' she asked Miss Heron.

'No,' said Miss Heron. 'Or we'll be here all night.'

When the ball was finally retrieved, it was Carrington's turn to bat. He was tall and blond and, according to Rose, looked like a young Leslie Howard. Carrington flexed his muscles and grinned round at the team. Justice saw Rose, who was meant to be fielding, waving at him.

Justice was ashamed of herself for hoping Carrington would miss but there was a sharp crack as he made contact. The ball shot straight at a birdwatching Henry. In slow motion, Justice watched Henry raise his hands and catch the ball. His glasses fell off but he managed to throw it to Salim, who was guarding the post.

'Out!' shouted Miss Heron.

*

By the time the Defenders came to bat, they had quite an audience. Hutchins, Miss Morris – accompanied by her dog Sabre – Miss Bathurst, Mrs Hopkirk the housekeeper. Even Major Hammond. The major was watching the game with his arms folded and a frown knitting his bushy eyebrows together. Justice wondered what he thought about the way the St Wilfred's boys were chatting and laughing with the Highbury House girls. Miss de Vere had wanted the two schools to get together in a 'civilised' way, but Justice thought that the major would prefer the previous uncivilised arrangement.

But there was no doubt that the rounders match had changed things. Justice found herself talking to two boys called Green and Malone. They seemed almost human and Justice liked the way that Green rolled his eyes when he mentioned Carrington. Eva congratulated Henry on his catch (Henry blushed bright red), and Nora was making a group of boys laugh with her impersonations.

It was more peaceful being a fielder but Justice knew that she had to keep alert in case, like Henry, she was called upon to make a crucial catch. It was a beautiful autumn afternoon, the grass – despite Hutchins' best efforts – carpeted with leaves. The sun was warm but, standing still, wearing only a short-sleeved aertex top and sports skirt, made Justice feel slightly chilly. She jogged over to the edge of the field and saw Miss de Vere hurrying towards the match. Was the headmistress going to watch? No, she went up to Miss Morris and Miss Bathurst. The three of them had a whispered conversation and then they all headed back towards the school, Sabre trotting importantly behind them. What was going on?

'Justice!'

The ball was coming towards her. Unlike Henry, Justice missed completely but it didn't matter too much. She picked the ball up and threw it to one of the closer fielders.

'Rounder!' shouted someone.

Rose made half a rounder, prancing past with her golden ponytail glowing in the sun. Carrington, who was standing near Justice, wolf-whistled. Alicia scored a rounder. Eva and Nora both missed. When it came to the last batter, Henry himself, the Defenders were on equal points. If he scored a rounder, they would tie with the Lightning Bolts. If he missed, Justice's team would win.

'We've got it in the bag,' said Carrington to Justice. 'Anderson's a complete rabbit.'

Justice found herself praying that Henry would score. He approached the square, glasses slightly askew. Moira, a fearsome bowler, threw the ball. Henry struck it hard and set off at a gallop. The ball, to Justice's relief, went towards Carrington, who lunged and missed. Henry completed the circle to rousing cheers.

'Equal points each,' said Miss Heron. 'Well played.'

And so it remained, even after both teams had been in for a second innings. The girls changed in the gymnasium and walked back to the school, past the vegetable garden that had replaced the tennis courts. Everyone was in good spirits. Justice knew that she should have been disappointed that her team didn't win but, actually, a draw seemed the best possible result. She was also delighted for Henry who, after his catch and his rounder, was the star of the day.

When they got back to the house, they expected to go to the refectory for orange squash and biscuits. The St Wilfred's boys were already in there, by the sound of it. But Miss Morris met them at the door and told them to go into the library. She looked strange, thought Justice. Red-eyed. Almost as if she'd been crying.

The rest of the school was already in the library, crowded together, pressed up against the bookshelves. Justice supposed that they couldn't use the assembly hall because the boys' desks were in there.

Miss de Vere was sitting at the librarian's table. She stood up when the fifth formers came in. Everyone fell silent.

Miss de Vere's face was very white. 'Girls,' she said. 'I'm afraid I've got some very bad news. I've just heard that Monsieur Pierre has been killed in France. He died for his country. He is a hero.'

CHAPTER 10

Justice remembered once before, when a teacher had died, how the whole school had seemed to go into shock. This time it was the same, only worse, because people had genuinely liked the French teacher.

'I keep thinking about how he gave me that book to remember him by,' said Dorothy, her eyes red. 'I'll think of him every time I read it.'

They were sitting in Dorothy's room the day after the rounders match. It was prep time and dark outside, but Dorothy being head girl meant that Justice could visit her without getting into trouble. Justice was still on kitchen duties, so she'd managed to sneak up two cups of cocoa. The drink was rather cold by the time she'd got to the second floor but, combined with home-made biscuits from Dorothy's mother, it felt like a treat.

'I feel guilty about laughing at his accent,' said Justice. 'Though I'm sure it was put on half the time.'

'I think it was,' said Dorothy. 'He could speak several languages perfectly. Miss de Vere told me. She's very upset.'

Justice remembered how, on a previous adventure, she had suspected the headmistress of conspiring with Monsieur Pierre. They were just friends, she realised now.

'Do you know how he died?' she asked.

'No,' said Dorothy. 'But I think he may have been a spy. I heard Miss de Vere talking to Miss Morris. She said something about "Jean-Maurice working undercover". That must mean spying.'

'I wrote to my dad about Monsieur Pierre,' said Justice. 'He might know something.'

'Are you looking forward to seeing your dad on the half holiday?' asked Dorothy.

'I really am,' said Justice. 'I always miss him but this term it seems worse. Everything seems so uncertain suddenly.'

'I know,' said Dorothy. 'I wish there was a new mystery to take our minds off things.'

This was where Justice could help. She told Dorothy about the face at the window in the North Turret.

'I can't think how he got up there. I mean, it's miles from the ground.'

'A ladder?' suggested Dorothy.

'I looked and there was nothing there. Well, there was a ledge, Henry said. But, even if the man had been standing on the ledge, where did he disappear to?'

'Let's go and explore,' said Dorothy. 'It's better than sitting here feeling sad.'

Justice couldn't help smiling. Her friend might be head girl and wear her hair up but she was still the old intrepid, mystery-solving Dorothy. And, because Dorothy was no longer a maid but an important school personage, they could almost go wherever they pleased.

The building was quiet but Justice knew that, in about fifteen minutes, the dormy bells would ring and the corridors would be full of chatter and clatter. As they passed Matron's room they could hear the wireless playing the Louis Armstrong song, 'Jeepers Creepers'. Dorothy and Justice crossed the landing and climbed the stairs to the attic rooms. The door to Dorothy's old room was firmly shut but, when they approached the turret, they heard the low murmur of a voice.

The girls edged closer. There was a faint line of light showing beneath the door. Justice remembered that this room didn't have any blackout blinds, probably because it was empty most of the time. Trying to be as quiet as possible, she peered through the keyhole.

Mr Hoffman was talking on the telephone.

Justice didn't know what language he was speaking.

But she thought it might be German.

The dormy bell made Justice and Dorothy jump. They sprinted back along the passage. Justice knew that Mr Hoffman would soon be on his way to supervise the boys' dormitories. Not that he did it very well.

The radio was still playing 'Jeepers Creepers'. Dorothy and Justice had a whispered chat on the landing.

'He was talking German,' said Justice.

'People in the village are saying that Mr Hoffman's a German spy,' said Dorothy. 'Someone spat at him in the high street. My dad said it was a disgrace.'

'That's awful,' said Justice.

'I know,' said Dorothy. 'All the same, we ought to keep watching him.'

Matron's door opened. 'Better get moving, Justice,' she said. 'Unless you want to be late for dormy. Again.'

'Yes, Matron,' said Justice, meekly. Then with a 'See you later,' to Dorothy, she headed back to Barnowls.

Justice was the first one in the dormitory for a change. Eva had left some drawings out on her bed. Justice went to look at them.

'What are you doing?' Eva's voice came from the doorway.

'Just looking . . .'

'Well, don't.' Eva crossed the room, snatched up the pages and put them in her locker.

'Sorry,' said Justice.

For a second Eva glared at her, then her face relaxed and she looked like her old self again. 'It's OK. It's just that they're not very good. I don't want people looking at them.'

'I understand. I'm sorry. I'd hate anyone to look at my journal.'

'As if anyone would be interested.' Rose was amongst them. 'Now, my latest love letter from Carrington – that *does* make interesting reading.' Eva and Nora gathered around Rose to hear more. This gave Justice a chance to talk to Stella and Letitia.

'There's some mystery,' she said. 'It's to do with Mr Hoffman. I'll tell you about it tomorrow.'

'I like Mr Hoffman,' said Letitia. 'He's better than that awful major.'

'Anyone is,' said Stella.

'I think Mr Hoffman might be German,' said Justice.

'Of course he is,' said Stella. 'Hoffman's a German name. *Tales of Hoffmann* and all that.'

Justice stared. She'd never thought about where the name came from. Some detective she'd make.

'He was talking on the phone in German,' she said. She wanted her friends to be interested and intrigued. She wanted them to have a mystery to solve to take their minds off Monsieur Pierre and the awfulness of war.

'Probably talking to his mother,' said Stella. 'Things are pretty dangerous for some people in Germany, you know.'

Justice had no answer to this and, a few seconds later, Rose told her to close her mouth in case a fly flew into it.

CHAPTER 11

On Saturdays the fifth years had lessons as usual in the morning but the afternoon was free, supposedly for revision. For the lower school, Saturday afternoons were devoted to games. The second and third years had lacrosse matches and it seemed that most of the school was either playing, or on the touchlines of the top field cheering the players on. Justice, Stella and Letitia were able to sneak away into the grounds behind the school.

'If anyone asks,' said Justice, 'we can say that we want to revise somewhere peaceful.'

'I ought to watch the second half of the match,' said Stella. 'Sarah's playing.'

'It won't take long,' said Justice.

They brought their books with them, just in case, but no

one challenged them as they left by the scullery door and walked through the formal gardens. When Justice had first arrived at Highbury House, these had been rather beautiful, full of roses and neat flower beds. But now the flowers were all dead and weeds were growing between the paving slabs. A hen coop was where the ornamental fountain used to be. The statue of a fish was still there but water no longer flowed out of its mouth. There was no gardener at the school these days and Hutchins had better things to do – growing vegetables and looking after the pigs and the hens.

'Let's go to the Old Barn,' said Letitia. 'We won't be overheard there.'

It was typical of Letitia, thought Justice, that she'd choose the place where they had had a terrifying experience two years ago.

As they skirted the woods on their way to the barn, they saw a flash of blonde hair disappearing into the trees.

'That's Rose,' said Letitia. 'She's on her way to see Carrington. I heard her telling Alicia at breakfast.'

Justice thought of the former head girl, Helena Bliss, who'd had a habit of meeting people in the grounds. Rose was rather like Helena, and had a similar ability to flout the rules without getting caught.

It was quite cosy in the barn. They sat on hay bales and

Justice produced some rather crumbly biscuits, the last of Dad's tuck box. A couple of the hens, who were allowed to roam freely in the daytime, pecked around their feet.

'It doesn't seem possible that there's a war on,' said Letitia.

'It probably seems possible to Monsieur Pierre's family,' said Stella. This had the effect of silencing them all. Justice knew that Stella's family had relatives in Europe. The phony war was not phony to them.

Justice thought it was time to change the subject. 'So,' she said, 'I've got three mysteries for you.' She told them about seeing the face in the window of the North Turret, about Dorothy hearing voices there, and Mr Hoffman talking on the phone in German. It was the first that caught her friends' imaginations.

'How could that be?' said Stella. 'It's so high off the ground.'

'Maybe he was a parachutist,' giggled Letitia. There had been lots of scare stories in the newspapers about German parachutists – often disguised as nuns, for some reason – descending on the English countryside.

'I did wonder if he was hanging from something,' said Justice, 'but when I looked out of the window, there was nothing.'

'There must have been something,' said Stella. She had a very practical mind (she wanted to be a doctor) and it upset her when she couldn't find logical explanations.

'There was a narrow ledge,' said Justice. 'He could have been standing on that. But where did he disappear to?'

'And you didn't recognise the face?' said Letitia.

'I only saw him for a few seconds,' said Justice. 'I would almost have thought I'd imagined the whole thing if Henry hadn't been there too.'

'Did Henry recognise him?' asked Stella.

'He said he didn't. We need to try and get a description written down but we haven't had time to talk it over, what with the rounders match and Monsieur Pierre and everything.'

'Henry did really well in the rounders match,' said Letitia.

'He did,' said Justice. 'But I saw him yesterday, just for a few minutes, and he said that Carrington was being even nastier to him.'

'Typical,' said Letitia. 'Carrington's a bully. I can't think what Rose sees in him.'

'Shh,' said Stella suddenly. 'Did you hear that?'

'What?' whispered Justice.

'I thought I heard someone outside.'

Justice tiptoed to the door and looked out. A wind was stirring the treetops and gusts of leaves blew across the lawn. She could hear the pigs grunting in their sty and, a long way off, shouts from the playing fields. But there was nobody to be seen. She remembered the time, two years ago, when the Barnowls had thought that they'd seen a ghost in the garden, a spectral figure of a woman dressed in white. That apparition had turned out to be all too human.

She went back inside the barn. 'I can't see anyone.'

'I thought I heard someone moving about,' said Stella.

'Maybe it was just the wind,' said Justice, 'or the hens.' Two of the hens were now watching them from the rafters.

'Maybe it was the phantom parachutist,' said Letitia.

Justice shivered, despite herself. 'I'll talk to Dad about it on the half holiday,' she said.

'No point asking mine,' said Letitia. 'He'll just say "stuff and nonsense".' She imitated Lord Blackstock's gruff tones.

'My mum will ask if I've been eating cheese late at night,' said Stella.

The girls laughed but, on the way back, Justice thought to look at the long grass around the barn.

It was flattened, as if someone had been walking over it.

CHAPTER 12

Like everything else, the half holiday was a bit different this term. Lots of parents couldn't come, and those that did looked different somehow. This was partly because some of the fathers were in uniform. Rose's father wasn't but he still swept into the refectory as if he owned it. Rose's mother was as glamorous as ever in a big fur coat. 'Innocent animals died to make that,' Justice's mother would have said. Letitia's father, Lord Blackstock, who *did* partly own the school, was in his usual old tweed jacket.

'The army wouldn't have him,' said Letitia, as Justice walked over to speak to the Blackstocks. Because of a previous adventure, their two families were on very good terms.

'That's what my dad said too,' said Justice.

'I'm too old and cranky,' said Lord Blackstock, with his sudden unexpected laugh. 'But your father is still a young man.'

Justice felt a tiny twinge of fear.

Justice kept watching the door for her dad. And then, beside her, she heard Stella give a sudden exclamation. Stella's parents had entered the room accompanied by a tall young man in uniform: Stella's brother, Josh.

Sarah rushed over to greet him, chattering all the time.

Stella clutched Justice's arm. 'How can Josh be in the army? He's only seventeen.'

'Let's go and ask,' said Justice.

Sarah was still talking but Josh turned to say hallo to Justice and Stella. Justice had only met him once before. He seemed nice but very shy.

'Why are you in uniform?' asked Stella, her voice sounding so sharp that Sarah actually stopped in mid-monologue.

'Calm down, sis,' said Josh. 'I'm only a cadet. I thought you'd like to see me in uniform.'

'I think he looks very smart,' said Sarah.

Stella said nothing.

'Hallo, Justice.' In all the excitement, Justice had missed her father's entrance. She gave him a huge hug.

'You're late.'

'Sorry. I got caught up with something at work. Shall we be off?'

Miss de Vere and Major Hammond were in the great hall, greeting the parents. It was half holiday for the boys too, although the two schools were being kept apart as usual. The boys' parents were ushered into the assembly hall and the girls' into the refectory. Justice saw Carrington going past with his parents and two brothers who looked like smaller versions of him. *Fancy there being three of him*, thought Justice. She hoped that she would see Henry's parents.

'Herbert!'

'Dolores.'

Justice groaned inwardly. She could never like the fact that her father and Miss de Vere were friends. She had to stand there awkwardly while they chatted, Miss de Vere's red-nailed hand on Herbert's arm. She introduced him to Major Hammond and the two men shook hands. The major asked where they were going and Herbert said, 'Jury's Gap' – a nearby beach.

'You'll get wet,' said Miss de Vere. It had been raining all morning.

'We don't mind that, do we, Justice?' said Herbert.

'No,' said Justice. 'Shall we go now?'

All three adults laughed, although Justice thought that the major gave her a sharp look. Then, thank goodness, they were free of the school. For an afternoon, at least.

Even Jury's Gap wasn't the same. There was barbed wire to stop you going on to the beach and the sand and the sea were the same dreary grey colour. Herbert and Justice walked along the coastal path for about half an hour, then retreated to a nearby pub, The Singing Sands, for lunch.

Justice cheered up eating fish and chips and drinking ginger beer. The landlord told them that he'd caught the fish himself and his wife grew the potatoes.

'Can you still fish here?' asked Dad.

'Yes,' said the landlord. 'If you know where to look. I'm on coastal patrol, you see. In case of invasion. I know the Kent coast like the back of my hand. My wife and I have lived here all our lives.'

'The seas are rough,' said Dad.

'But the harbours are safe,' replied the man.

In case of invasion. For almost the first time, Justice thought about how close they were to mainland Europe. A few miles away, in Dover, you could see the coast of France on a clear day. But surely the Germans would never invade

France? There was something called the Maginot Line that was meant to be impossible for them to cross. Justice didn't want to think about the war so she told Dad about the rounders match. He laughed at the description of Henry's now-famous catch.

'Sounds like you and Henry did well,' said Herbert. 'Sport can bring people together.'

'Sometimes,' said Justice, thinking of the footballers shouting at Henry when he missed the ball. 'Sometimes it can make things worse.'

She had been going to tell Dad about the face at the window and the voices in the North Turret but somehow she didn't. She wanted to enjoy their day together without thinking about mysteries. Or the war.

They did discuss Monsieur Pierre briefly.

'Poor Jean-Maurice,' said Herbert. 'He was a brave man. Dolores is very upset.'

Justice decided to forgive her father the first names, just this once.

'Belgium is a dangerous place at the moment,' said Herbert.

'Belgium?' said Justice. 'I thought he was killed in France?'

'Yes. France. Sorry.'

There was a brief silence. Justice drained her ginger beer. 'Did you see Rose's father?' she asked. 'Swanking about the place. Rose goes on as if he's winning the war single-handed but, only a few years ago, she said that he admired Hitler.'

'Lots of the English upper classes did,' said Herbert. 'But it's better not to mention the fact. Do you want a pudding?'

Justice knew he was changing the subject but she *did* want a pudding so she let it go.

All too soon, they were driving back to Highbury House.

It was still raining and almost dark but Justice could see a greenish glimmer on the horizon. She thought of a story she'd heard about strange lights on the marshland at night. 'The devil's lights', people called them. 'If you follow the lights and leave the path,' a local farmer had once told Justice, 'then you're lost.' She was glad of their trusty car, Bessie, and of Dad's solid presence at the wheel.

Dad parked outside the school and they went into the shelter of the porch to say goodbye. Another family had the same idea. A mother and father and a boy with glasses.

'Hallo, Jones. Fancy seeing you here.'

Henry's parents seemed nice, Justice was pleased to see. 'I'm so glad to meet you,' said Henry's mother. 'You've made a real difference to Hen.'

'Mum!' groaned Henry. 'Don't use that name.'

'Sorry.' His mother gave him a quick hug and smiled at Justice. Justice smiled back but she felt the familiar ache that always struck her heart when she met people's mothers. It wasn't that she minded her friends having nice mothers; it was just that it made her miss her own.

The Andersons went inside to talk to Major Hammond and Justice and her dad were left alone.

'Bye, Dad,' said Justice, trying to sound cheerful. 'See you at Christmas.'

Dad gave her a fierce hug. 'Bye, darling. And Justice?'

'What?'

For a moment, it seemed as if Dad had something more to say but then he just hugged her again and said, 'Nothing. See you at Christmas.'

The car soon disappeared into the rain but Justice stood watching until the bell rang for Meal.

CHAPTER 13

The day after the half holiday was always a bit miserable. At least it was Saturday, which meant a free afternoon. The fifth years were on garden duties so, after breakfast, they went out and collected carrots and beetroot. The vegetable patch also contained huge pumpkins that reminded Justice that it would be Halloween in a week's time.

Rose complained about getting her hands dirty but Justice liked picking vegetables. There was something satisfying about pulling them out of the earth and it was good to be outside, even though the morning was misty and cold. Stella and Eva were collecting eggs. Eva screamed because she said that a hen was giving her nasty looks. Letitia threw a mouldy carrot at her.

They washed their hands in the scullery and went

upstairs for maths with Miss Morris. It still seemed wrong to do lessons at the weekend but Justice was looking forward to a free afternoon. She was trying to work out a very tricky equation when there was a knock at the door.

'Please, miss.' It was a first year on messenger duties. 'Can Justice Jones go to Miss de Vere's office?'

Everyone looked as Justice got up. Stella smiled encouragingly. Justice tried to think of any school rules she had broken recently but, rather disappointingly, nothing came to mind. She started to feel the first icy touch of fear.

Miss de Vere's study seemed very full. Slowly, and with increasing dread, Justice noted the presence of Peter's mother, Miss Heron and a policeman she recognised called Inspector Deacon.

'Please sit down, Justice,' said Miss de Vere. 'You will need to be very brave, my dear. It's about your father.'

The room swam in front of Justice's eyes. Peter's mother came to sit next to her and placed her hand on Justice's arm. Miss Heron was also there, hovering supportively.

Miss de Vere's voice seemed to come from very far away. 'The alarm was raised when Herbert didn't keep a dinner engagement with Mr and Mrs Patterson last night.' Mr and

Mrs Patterson were Peter's parents. 'This morning his car was found at Headcorn airfield. Given that he didn't get in contact with the Pattersons, the police are afraid that Herbert might have been abducted.'

This word finally registered with Justice. 'Abducted? Why would he be abducted?'

Inspector Deacon spoke for the first time. 'We have reason to believe that your father was involved in important espionage work.'

Oh, Dad. For a moment, Justice felt quite furious with her father. He had promised her that he wouldn't get involved in anything dangerous. So much for carrying on with his legal work and being an air raid warden. He was all she had and now he was gone.

She only realised that she was crying when the tears fell on to her lap.

Peter's mother, Hilda, patted her shoulder. 'I promised Herbert that you'd always have a home with us, Justice. We'll look after you.'

'You promised him?' Justice looked up, rubbing her eyes. 'Did you know about this?'

'Not exactly,' said Hilda. 'But he came to see us a few days ago and asked us to look after you if . . . if anything happened to him.'

Justice remembered saying goodbye to Dad in the porch, and how he had seemed to want to say something to her but then had changed his mind. Had he known that he was going into danger? She realised that Inspector Deacon was speaking.

'There's no need to despair, Justice. I've got my best men on the case and I'm hopeful that we can find Mr Jones. They're combing the area around Headcorn as we speak.'

'If Bessie . . . his car . . . was found at an airfield,' said Justice. 'Do you think he's been taken abroad? On a plane?'

'That's a line of enquiry,' said Inspector Deacon. 'Now, Justice. We've worked together before. I know you're a brave girl. You've got to stay strong. You can get through this. I know you can.'

Veritas et fortitudo, Dad used to say at the end of his letters. *Truth and courage.* The thought that she might never see his handwriting again was too much for Justice, and she burst into fresh tears.

Miss Heron took Justice to the fifth-form common room. 'I'll fetch Stella to come and sit with you,' she said. Peter's mother had gone home, after hugging Justice and promising to stay in touch. Justice was glad that she'd left. Hilda was nice, if a bit fussy, but she wasn't Justice's mum. She wasn't anything to do with Justice, really. In a strange way, it was easier to be at Highbury House. At least she was with people who knew her and who understood about Dad.

Miss Heron must have told Stella because she came straight in and put her arms around Justice.

'I'm so sorry,' she said.

Stella was being so kind but, after a few minutes, Justice felt an overwhelming desire to escape. She just wanted to be on her own for a bit, to think about what had happened and to cry in peace. She told Stella that she needed something from the dormy but, instead of going upstairs via the maids' stairs, Justice crept out of the scullery door and into the garden.

The hens were squawking from the top of their coop but there were no pupils or teachers within sight. Lessons were still going on, then it would be lunchtime. Justice remembered, years ago, going into the barn to cry. What had she been upset about then? She could hardly remember. Something trivial, she was sure. Nothing like losing your only parent.

Justice's feeling of loss was so great that, when she reached the safety of the barn, she couldn't cry at first. She sat, dry-eyed, on a hay bale and thought about Dad. Why had he got involved with what Inspector Deacon called 'espionage work'? Why had he asked Peter's parents to look after her? Didn't he care at all? Then she remembered Dad's face when he'd said goodbye to her yesterday.

'*Bye, darling. And Justice?*'

'*What?*'

'*Nothing. See you at Christmas.*'

Justice let out a cry that was almost a wail and threw herself on the ground to sob. She only stopped because a hen came right up to her face, looking at her with its strange dinosaur head on one side. Justice could hear other hens scrabbling about in the hay. Then she heard another sound.

Breathing. Human breathing.

Justice got up and went to the door. There was no one outside. She thought of the other day, when she'd been in the barn with Letitia and Stella, and the grass had been flattened as if someone had been walking there. Now, there were no signs that anyone except the hens had come near the place. Even so, Justice had the strangest feeling that she was being watched.

Back at the house, the girls were going into lunch, chattering about the possibility of the food being slightly nicer than usual, i.e. edible. Justice hovered in the scullery corridor. She didn't want to talk to anyone and she certainly didn't want to eat anything.

'Justice!' said a voice.

It was Dorothy. Like Stella, she obviously already knew because she gave Justice a hug and said, 'Want to come up to my room? I've got biscuits.'

'Yes, please,' said Justice.

Justice knew that Dorothy was probably upset too. She was very fond of Justice's dad. He had made it possible for her to be a pupil at Highbury House and not a maid.

But when they were in Dorothy's bedroom and sitting on the patchwork quilt, Dorothy said, 'So, are we going to solve this mystery?'

And Justice felt the weight on her heart lift a little. After all, they'd only found Dad's car. Not Dad himself. She remembered in one of Mum's books – *Murder in the Mansion*, she thought – Leslie Light saying, 'If there's no body, we can't assume there's been a murder.' She had to assume that Dad was still alive somewhere.

'It's a tragedy,' she'd heard Hilda saying to Miss de Vere. But it wasn't a tragedy. Not yet anyway. It was a mystery.

And mysteries were what Justice was good at.

CHAPTER 14

Miss de Vere said that Justice could miss church the next day. 'You can just sit and read if you like. Stella can stay with you.' Justice had often dreamed of missing church to stay in bed and read but, today, she found that she didn't want to be alone. She wanted to be in the line of girls walking into the village, complaining about the cold and the boredom of the service. Even Stella, who often said that she shouldn't be made to go to church because she was Jewish, agreed. 'It's better to be doing something, even if it's walking half a mile in the freezing cold.'

Everyone was being very nice to Justice. Rose gave her a quick hug before handing over a note from Henry, delivered via Carrington.

Dear Jones. I'm so sorry but don't give up! We can solve this. Love H

Justice read this out and Eva burst into tears. 'That's so sweet.'

Henry wasn't in the line of boys following the girls to church. 'Carrington says he's got asthma,' said Rose, her tone picking up the contempt of the person who had given her the message.

'Poor Henry,' said Stella. 'Asthma's horrid. My brother Josh gets it.'

Even at church, the verger smiled sympathetically at Justice. He was a strange-looking man, youngish but with a very wrinkled face. He walked with a heavy limp and there were lots of rumours at Highbury House about how he had got the injury: fighting off a wild animal, a circus injury, rescuing a child from a runaway horse, flying a plane in the First World War. But today he gave Justice a wink as he passed her a hymn book. The vicar, the Reverend Percy Snodgrass, was above such things but he did pray for 'the sick, the dead and the missing' during the service. *Does he mean Dad?* wondered Justice. She had to fight to stop herself crying.

Stella squeezed her hand.

Back at Highbury House, they had hot chocolate and biscuits. 'It's the last of the cocoa,' said Cook, when she handed them their cups. 'There's a war on, you know.' Grown-ups had taken to saying this, Justice noticed, as if anyone was likely to forget.

Justice, Stella and Letitia took their cocoa to Dorothy's room for a meeting. Dorothy had even started a plan, the way Justice always did with a new mystery.

> *The Disappearance of Herbert Jones*
> *Clues*
> *The car*
> *Headcorn*
> *Miss de Vere – what does she know?*
> *Mysterious voices in North Turret*
> *The face at the window*

'Belgium,' said Justice, after studying the list in silence for a few minutes.

'Belgium?' repeated Dorothy.

'Dad said that Monsieur Pierre was killed in Belgium, and Miss de Vere said it was France. Maybe Dad knew more about it than he let on? Maybe they were in the same group of spies. Inspector Deacon said that Dad was involved in espionage work. That means spying.' Justice thought for a moment. 'Dorothy, you said you thought Monsieur Pierre might have been a spy. Didn't Miss de Vere say he was involved in undercover work?'

'Yes,' said Dorothy. 'Though when I tried to ask her about it, just casually, she pretended I'd misunderstood. But I think it was true. After all, Monsieur Pierre spoke all those languages. And he gave me that book. It's about a man called Lupin who keeps disguising himself.'

'Our only real clue is the car,' said Letitia. 'I wish we could examine it. I wonder if it's still at the airfield?'

'There's only one way to find out,' said Dorothy. 'Let's go there.'

The three fifth formers stared at her. 'How?' said Stella at last.

'It's right over the other side of Kent,' said Justice. 'I looked on a map last night. If we went by train it would take hours. There aren't many trains running on the branch lines now. I heard Cook talking about it the other day.'

'We could drive,' said Dorothy.

'How?' said Justice. 'No one has a car and none of us can drive.'

'I can,' said Dorothy.

Once again, the younger girls stared at her. It was as if Dorothy were growing more grown-up by the second, thought Justice.

'Dad taught me in the holidays,' said Dorothy. 'And Miss Morris has a car. She gets petrol because she's an air raid warden. She's let me borrow it a few times. I can ask if I can take Justice for a drive. To take her mind off things.'

'You mean go now?' said Justice.

'Why not?' said Dorothy.

In the end it was surprisingly easy. Miss de Vere and Miss Morris both said yes immediately. Stella and Letitia stayed behind to continue investigations. They were planning to 'shadow' Mr Hoffman.

After lunch – rissoles like tiny bullets – Dorothy and Justice set out in Miss Morris's green Morris Oxford.

'Do you think she bought the car because it's got the same name as her?' said Dorothy, as they drove through the gates with the stone griffins on either side.

'It's not her real name, though, is it?' said Justice. They had discovered this on a previous adventure. Justice was feeling very strange. On one hand, it was exciting to be escaping from school, even just for an afternoon. She kept looking at Dorothy's profile as she drove and wondering how her friend had become so competent all of a sudden. It was fun to see the marsh stretching on either side of them, to look at the map with the route to Headcorn sketched in red, and to eat toffees from a tin thoughtfully provided by Letitia. But, all the time, there was a voice in Justice's head saying: *Dad is gone, you might never see him again.* The thought made her feel sick and faint, though that could have partly been to do with Dorothy's habit of taking corners very fast.

The marshes gave way to fields and woodland. They passed through lots of little villages, all looking very quiet on this Sunday afternoon in wartime. The signposts were painted over (supposedly to confuse enemy troops in case of invasion) but Justice was following the names on the map: Snargate, Appledore, Tenterden, Biddenden. As they got nearer to Headcorn, Justice felt her stomach tying itself in knots. What would they find? Armed Germans waiting to shoot them? Angry Home Guards telling them to go back?

When, after over an hour's driving, Dorothy turned a corner and they found themselves in an almost empty field, the two girls looked at each other. 'Is this it?'

Justice had been to Croydon airport with her dad once. He had been meeting some of his old Royal Flying Corps friends and Justice remembered the huge planes, propellers whirring, the pilots with their leather caps shouting 'Chocks away!' Justice was meant to have gone up in one of the four-winged monsters but, at the last minute, she had felt too scared: Dad's friends had kept talking about 'looping the loop' and something called 'the flying fortress'. It had suddenly seemed absolutely necessary to stay on the ground. Dad hadn't minded. He'd just laughed and said he didn't blame her.

But Headcorn was nothing like Croydon. There were no planes, for one thing, just a concrete strip that might have been a runway, and a large barn with 'Keep Out' painted on it. But there, in the shadow of the hedge, was Bessie, Herbert's beloved Lagonda. It made Justice feel like crying to see it waiting there, like a charger awaiting its master's return from battle.

Dorothy parked next to Bessie and sighed with relief. 'We're here.'

'Well done,' said Justice. 'You're a brilliant driver.'

'Thank you,' said Dorothy. 'It's the longest drive I've done. I've hardly ever been in a proper car. I learnt on Dad's tractor.'

Justice was glad that she didn't know this before they set out.

She didn't expect Dad's car to be unlocked but it was. Was this in itself suspicious? Herbert always locked it. There was a book face down on the passenger seat. The *Complete Works of Shakespeare*.

'Strange thing to have in a car,' said Dorothy.

'Dad takes it everywhere,' said Justice. 'He loves Shakespeare. He and Mum used to have this game where they quoted things to each other. "Screw your courage to the sticking place" – that was one of Mum's favourites.' She'd been saying to herself ever since she'd got the news about Dad.

'*Macbeth*,' said Dorothy. 'What play was your dad reading?'

Justice turned the book over. One page was turned down.

'*King Lear*,' she said. 'That's funny.'

'It's not particularly funny,' said Dorothy. 'I'm doing it for Highers.'

'No, I mean Dad never keeps his place by turning the page down. Mum used to say that it was like assaulting the book.'

Justice looked at the page with the corner turned down. One line had been underlined in pencil. Justice knew that neither of her parents would ever write in a book. *Curiouser and curiouser.*

<u>Kent:</u> *See better, Lear; and let me still remain*
 The true blank of thine eye.

Justice had the familiar feeling that Shakespeare was saying something that she didn't quite understand. *See better . . . The true blank of thine eye.* What did that mean? Only 'Kent' and a bit of 'see' had been underlined. Was this an anagram of some kind, a word puzzle where the letters could be rearranged to spell something different?

Dorothy was walking around the car. 'There's mud on the wheels. But then it was raining hard on Friday, wasn't it?'

Justice remembered walking along the beach in the rain with her dad; sitting in the pub eating fish and chips while the squall battered against the windows; watching Bessie's tail lights disappear into the darkness.

Justice looked at the driver's seat. It was drawn forward, close to the steering wheel. Dad was proud of the car's adjustable seats and always had his pushed back to accommodate his long legs. 'Someone else has been driving the car,' she said.

'They must have driven him here and then taken him somewhere else,' said Dorothy. 'But where?'

Justice looked around the empty field. Inspector Deacon had said that his men were combing the area but there was no sign of them today. Was this because they knew Dad was somewhere else? Maybe even abroad?

'Let's go and explore the barn,' said Justice. But she took the *Complete Works of Shakespeare* with her, the page still carefully folded back.

CHAPTER 15

Tailing someone, thought Stella, was harder than it sounded. As it was Sunday, they had a free afternoon. The boys and girls were not meant to mix but Stella saw Rose and Alicia heading to the woods with Carrington and Meek. Some of the other boys were playing cricket on the top field, and Moira and Irene went to join in. Stella and Letitia, watching from a first-floor window, saw Moira hit the ball with her usual power. The fielders scurried into the trees to retrieve it.

'She'll be on the St Wilfred's cricket team soon,' said Letitia.

'But where's Mr Hoffman?' said Stella. 'Shouldn't he be umpiring or something?'

Normally, she would have been worried about following a teacher. She would have protested to Justice that teachers were trustworthy people, that they wouldn't be spies or involved in a crime. Justice, of course, thought everyone was a possible suspect. That was one of the things that made her a rather alarming best friend. But, today, Stella was determined to do Justice justice. She knew what Justice's dad meant to her: she often said that he was the only person she had in the world. 'You've got me and my family,' Stella always replied, but she knew it wasn't the same. Stella had her mum and her dad, all her brothers and sisters. She had so many people and look how worried she was about Josh joining the army. What if Josh was all she had and then he went missing?

Stella squared her shoulders. 'We have to find him,' she said. 'Let's look in the boys' dormitories, then go up to his room in the attic.'

The boys' dormitories were deserted and *very* tidy. The beds looked as if the sheets and blankets had been straightened by a ruler.

'I bet Major Hammond insists on everything being just so,' said Stella. 'He's even worse than Matron.'

'Where is the Mad Major today?' said Letitia.

'Apparently he went out in his car,' said Stella. 'Rose saw him leaving. You know he's got that little red sports car.'

'Let's hope he doesn't crash into Dorothy,' said Letitia.

They walked to the end of the corridor. The last room, the one where Stella and Justice had heard the wireless playing, was locked.

'Why's it locked?' said Letitia. 'There must be some mystery. If only we could get a spare key.'

'Hutchins has copies of all the keys,' said Stella, who'd once stolen them to save her friends.

'Let's see if we can sneak into his room later,' said Letitia. Stella's heart sank at the thought of more rule-breaking but she agreed. Anything to help Justice.

They climbed the stairs to the second floor. Matron's wireless was playing but there was no other sound as they tiptoed to the attic stairs. They could hear the sixth formers in their common room but there was no sound from Mr Hoffman's room. Letitia tried the door. Locked.

They looked at each other, frustrated.

'Shall we search the grounds?' said Stella.

'Let's go to the common room,' said Letitia. 'That'll give us a vantage point.'

The fifth-form common room was on the first floor, looking out over the grounds. There were a few girls in there, huddled up on the sofas, reading books or knitting. No one took much notice of Stella and Letitia as they knelt on the window seat and peered out. They could see Henry

Anderson, binoculars around his neck, heading for the woods to do some birdwatching, and Eva wandering along a path carrying her sketchbook. And – yes! – Mr Hoffman heading towards the house. As they watched he sat on a bench in the kitchen gardens, got out writing paper and pen, and started to write.

Letitia nodded towards the door and the girls silently left the room. On the landing, Letitia said, 'If we can get on to the flat roof by the scullery we'll be able to see what he's writing.'

'How can we get there?' said Stella.

'Through a window,' said Letitia. 'I did it the other day when I wanted to play a prank on Irene. I was going to play her violin on the roof but it was raining so no one came by.'

On the first-floor corridor, one of the sash windows was already half open. Matron believed in fresh air, even in October. Letitia stuck her head out, and about two feet below them was a flat rooftop.

'Shall I climb out?' she said.

'No,' said Stella. 'I'll do it.'

She felt that she owed it to Justice somehow.

Dorothy and Justice were doing their own detective work, prowling around the barn at Headcorn airfield, trying to find a place to look in.

'Here,' said Dorothy, pointing to a spot where one of the wooden slats had come loose.

Justice pressed her eye to the gap. There was still straw on the floor of the barn, as if the animals had only just left, but she could see the looming shapes of planes, some with four wings, some with two.

'They obviously do fly from here,' she said.

'But there's no one here now,' said Dorothy. 'We'd better go. It'll be getting dark soon.'

Soon they were bowling back through the empty country lanes. Justice felt very slightly better: she'd seen Bessie and she had an actual clue in the solid shape of the Shakespeare book on her lap. When Dorothy started to sing 'A-Tisket, A-Tasket', Justice joined in.

Then the car stopped.

'What's happening?' said Justice. 'Why have you stopped?'

'I'm not sure,' said Dorothy, 'but I *think* it's run out of petrol.'

It was a longer drop than Stella had expected. She landed awkwardly on her hands and knees.

'Are you OK?' hissed Letitia from above.

Stella gave her a thumbs-up, although her knees hurt quite badly. She crawled to the edge of the roof and looked

111

down. It was perfect. She could see the top of Mr Hoffman's head as he bent over his letter. Squinting, she could even see the words.

Leibe Mutti . . .

They didn't learn German at Highbury House but Stella could guess what this meant. *Dear Mum.* Mr Hoffman was writing to his mother. Stella remembered what she'd said when Justice had heard Mr Hoffman on the telephone: *'Probably talking to his mother.'* It looked as if she had been right.

'Stella! What are you doing up there?'

Hell's bells and buckets of blood! It was Eva. She was standing on the path below, sketchbook in hand, eyes wide in innocent enquiry. 'What are you doing on the roof? Are you stuck?'

Mr Hoffman looked up. He folded the letter and put it in his pocket.

'Come down, Stella,' he said, 'and let's have a little talk.'

CHAPTER 16

'What do you mean?' said Justice.

'I think that arrow there means petrol,' said Dorothy. 'And it's pointing to empty. I didn't realise it would take so much to get to Headcorn.'

Justice opened the door and got out. They were in a narrow lane where the trees met overhead. Mist was blowing towards them like smoke.

'Where are we?' she said.

'We've passed Old Romney village,' said Dorothy. 'We're only about two miles from the school.'

'Two miles!' Justice had often gone that far on cross-country runs but, suddenly, with the sky darkening and the fog thickening, it seemed an impossible distance.

'We'll have to leave the car here,' said Dorothy. 'Miss Morris will be furious.'

They locked the car and set off, Justice still carrying the book. It seemed to get dark almost immediately and the trees creaked overhead. Justice wished she'd brought her torch but that was back in the dormitory, with the rest of her detecting kit. She hadn't prepared well for this journey at all.

'A-tisket, a-tasket . . .' began Dorothy. But neither of them had the heart to continue the song and Dorothy's voice died away.

After about ten minutes, they reached a crossroads, the white signpost glowing in the gloom.

'Which way is it?' said Justice. The directions, like the village names earlier, had all been painted over.

'I think it's left,' said Dorothy.

'Listen!' said Justice, grabbing her friend's arm. 'What's that?'

Very slowly, Stella descended the stairs and went out into the grounds. Mr Hoffman was waiting in the kitchen garden. As she reached him, he started to walk without speaking. Not quite knowing what to do, Stella kept pace with him. As they reached the gate to the overgrown formal garden, now a hen coop, he said, 'I'm assuming from your surname, Stella, that your family is Jewish. Goldman is a Jewish name.'

Stella was surprised. She didn't know that Mr Hoffman even knew her name.

'Yes,' she said.

'I'm Jewish too,' said Mr Hoffman. 'But I'm also German. My parents came to England after the Great War. My father had fought in the German army and even got a medal for bravery but he saw the way things were going – the attacks on Jews, the rise of the Nazi party. Not many people were so quick to see. Mother and Father came to England in 1920. My brother and I were children. It was a hard time to be a German in England. People called us names, spat at us in the street. My father died soon afterwards. He was broken-hearted because he loved Germany. My brother and I learnt to speak English like natives but Mutti is still more comfortable with her mother tongue. That was why I was writing to her in German.'

Stella didn't know what to say. She knew that her parents still had family in Germany. She knew Jewish people were being forced into prison camps. Last year she'd heard her parents talking about *'Kristallnacht'*, a pretty-sounding word for a very ugly thing: a night in Germany when Jewish-owned shops and businesses had been destroyed. The

'Kristall', German for 'crystal', came from the shards of broken glass that had littered the pavements.

'I'm lucky to have this job,' said Mr Hoffman. 'I'm not allowed to join the army because I'm a foreigner, and lots of German and Austrian Jews in Britain have been locked up, imprisoned as enemy aliens. Imagine that – you escape from hell and then you're put into prison.'

'It doesn't seem fair,' said Stella.

Mr Hoffman laughed. 'The world isn't fair, Stella. You'll soon work that out. But the Germans aren't the enemy. The Nazis are the enemy.'

'Have you still got family there?' asked Stella. 'In Germany?'

Mr Hoffman was silent for a moment before replying. 'Aunts, uncles and cousins. I don't know if any of them are still alive.'

'My friend, Justice,' Stella blurted out. 'Her father's disappeared.'

'I know,' said Mr Hoffman. 'I heard about that. I'm sorry. And you're looking for the culprit? Do you think there's a spy at Highbury House?'

Stella knew that she was blushing. It sounded so stupid after hearing Mr Hoffman's story.

'I want to help Justice,' she said at last.

'You can help her by just being her friend,' said Mr

Hoffman. He laughed and pointed towards the hedge. Parts of Letitia were visible through the threadbare branches. 'There's your other friend, checking on you. Go and tell her that you're all right.'

'I will,' said Stella. 'Thank you.' And she darted off along the path.

'*Auf Wiedersehen,*' Mr Hoffman called after her.

Justice and Dorothy stared at each other. The sound was getting louder – a relentless, rhythmical beat. Years ago, Nora had told them the story of the Headless Horseman of the Marshes: 'You hear horses' hooves, you turn round and there's nothing there but, when you turn your head, the horseman is beside you . . .'

'Probably just a farmer and his cart,' said Dorothy uncertainly.

'It doesn't sound like a cart,' said Justice. 'It's going too fast.'

There was no point trying to run away so they waited by the side of the road. The hoof beats got louder and louder. Justice edged closer to Dorothy. The horse was almost beside them before they saw it, a white blaze appearing through the mist. Justice couldn't see the rider but there was a glowing light where its head should be.

'John!' shouted Dorothy.

The horse came to a halt. The rider lowered his lantern and Justice was looking up at Dorothy's fifteen-year-old brother, John.

'Dot!' said John. 'What are you doing here?'

'I was driving,' said Dorothy, 'and the car ran out of petrol.'

'We're walking back to school,' added Justice.

John seemed to notice her for the first time. 'Justice! I didn't see you there. How are you?'

'Fine,' said Justice. She didn't want to tell John about Dad in case she started crying again.

'What are you doing?' Dorothy asked John.

'I took Sinbad to the smithy for a new shoe,' said John. 'Took longer than expected.'

Justice reached over to pat Sinbad. He was huge, a real carthorse, kind eyes glowing in the light of the lamp. He smelled of stables and hay. 'He's gorgeous,' she said.

'And he's so clever,' said John. 'I'm teaching him to do tricks.'

'Shouldn't you be getting him back to the farm?' said Dorothy.

'I'll walk you back,' said John. 'It's a long way with no light.'

'There's no need,' said Dorothy. 'We know the way.'

'You're walking in the wrong direction,' said John. Justice could see the gleam of his teeth as he grinned at his sister.

Dorothy ignored this. 'We're fine,' she said.

But Justice was secretly relieved when John slid off the horse and walked with them to the crossroads and the right turning. With the solid animal between them, his hooves now making a steady, comforting sound, Justice felt much safer.

By the time the lights of Highbury House appeared, Dorothy's watch said half past eight. With a pang, Justice remembered her father giving Dorothy that watch when she passed her School Certificate. He'd promised one to Justice too.

'Will you get into trouble?' asked John.

'I think they'll understand,' said Dorothy. Though she sounded unconvinced.

'I'd better be going back,' said John. 'Can you give me a leg up, Dot?'

Dorothy made her hands into a step to that John could heave himself on to Sinbad's back. Justice had often mounted Rebel, Letitia's pony, the same way. She'd had several holidays with Letitia, staying in her grand old house, riding and exploring the grounds. It seemed a hundred years ago.

'Bye, Justice,' said John. 'Bye, Pie Face.' They heard Sinbad break into a canter, his hooves soft on the grass. Justice and Dorothy turned back to face the school.

'Let's get it over with,' said Dorothy.

Miss Morris and Miss de Vere were both furious, but Justice could tell that this was because they'd been so worried.

'Where am I going to get more petrol?' asked Miss Morris. 'There's a war on, you know.'

'I don't understand why you went so far,' said Miss de Vere, with one of her disconcertingly direct looks.

'We were just driving around,' said Dorothy. 'Trying to take Justice's mind off things.'

Both teachers softened immediately.

'Go to your dormy now, Justice,' said Miss de Vere. 'It'll be lights out soon.'

Justice hurried away, pleased that the headmistress had not asked why she was carrying the *Complete Works of Shakespeare.*

The Barnowls were obviously still on Operation Be Nice To Justice.

'Where have you been?' snapped Rose, changing her tone to add: 'We were worried about you.'

'I went for a drive with Dorothy,' said Justice, 'and the car broke down.'

She tried to signal to Letitia and Stella that she had more to say.

'That must have been super,' said Eva.

'Weren't you scared on the marshes in the dark?' asked Nora with a grin. 'Did you see the Headless Horseman?'

'As a matter of fact,' said Justice, 'we did.'

The story of meeting John lasted until they were all in bed.

'Dorothy's brother is quite good-looking, I seem to remember,' said Rose.

'His horse was lovely,' said Justice.

Letitia started to laugh and Eva joined in before succumbing to the inevitable attack of hiccoughs. Eva's hiccoughing was such a feature of dormy life that Justice now found it rather soothing.

Justice wasn't sure if she felt better or worse after her day with Dorothy. On one hand, they had seen the car. They knew that Dad had been in Headcorn, even if he hadn't driven himself there. But they were no nearer to finding Dad himself.

Justice couldn't face writing in her journal so, instead, she opened the heavy volume of Shakespeare. It opened at the place where the corner had been turned down. Surely it was a clue? Dad would never deface a book like that without good reason.

Justice read the lines again. They were doing *Julius Caesar* for School Certificate and she only had a vague idea of what happened in King Lear. She thought it was about a king who divided his kingdom between his three daughters, which sounded a bit like a fairy tale, but Dorothy had said dreadful things happened in the play and it was all very sad at the end.

> *Kent: See better, Lear; and let me still remain*
> *The true blank of thine eye.*
> *Lear: Now, by Apollo . . .*
> *Kent: Now, by Apollo, King,*
> *Thou swear'st thy gods in vain.*

Who *was* Kent and why was he arguing with the king? It looked as if she was going to have to go back and read from the beginning. But she was too sleepy tonight. Ever since she'd heard about Dad, Justice had felt incredibly tired. She just wanted to close her eyes and forget everything. But, when she did shut them, images and words came flooding into her mind.

Dad's car standing empty in the field.

Miss de Vere telling her to be brave.

Dad chatting to the landlord in the pub. *'I'm on coastal patrol, you see. In case of invasion. I know the Kent coast like the back of my hand . . .'*

'The seas are rough.'

'But the harbours are safe.'

Justice sat bolt upright in bed. She opened the book again. The lights were out now but she had her torch. It illuminated the page, the tiny black typeface on the thin white paper. Dad had really only underlined one word. Kent.

Was he simply trying to tell Justice that he was still in Kent?

CHAPTER 17

But, if Justice was right and her dad *was* in Kent, where did she start looking? Kent was a big place, as she and Dorothy had discovered on their drive. How could Justice and her friends search the whole county? And where would they start looking?

'We could go back to Headcorn,' said Dorothy, when the Find Herbert Group (Dorothy, Justice, Stella and Letitia) met in her bedroom on Monday night.

'How?' said Justice. 'We haven't got a car.' Miss Morris's car was back in its garage by the pigsties. The maths teacher had been very forgiving but Justice didn't think she'd be letting Dorothy behind the wheel again.

The only other teacher with transport was Major Hammond, and his sports car. 'Far too young for him,' Dorothy said disapprovingly.

'We could go on horseback,' said Letitia. 'I'll get Dad to bring Cloud and Rebel over to the school.'

'That sounds lovely,' said Justice. 'But where would we go?' The girls fell silent.

Justice looked at Dorothy's list.

The Disappearance of Herbert Jones

Clues

The car

Headcorn

Miss de Vere – what does she know?

Mysterious voices in North Turret

The face at the window

Belgium – how did Herbert know that's where M. Pierre was?

'We should add the *Complete Works of Shakespeare*,' Justice said. 'That was a clue. Dad must have left the book for someone to find.'

Dorothy wrote it down.

'And we've still got to find the spy,' said Letitia. 'Even if it's not Mr Hoffman.'

'I'm sure it isn't,' said Stella. She'd told the others about her conversation with the St Wilfred's master.

'Does your dad know anyone else at the school?' asked Letitia.

'Only Miss de Vere,' said Justice. Herbert had once defended Miss de Vere in a trial. They were friends, and sometimes Justice feared that the friendship would become something more. Try as she would, though, she couldn't see the headmistress as a spy.

'There's the connection with Monsieur Pierre,' said Dorothy. 'I'll see if I can find out more about him from Miss de Vere. I'll say I want to write to his family and say how sorry I am. Actually, I would like to do that.'

'What about the book he gave you?' said Justice. 'Lupin or whatever it was called. Could there be a clue in that?'

'Not all books have clues in, Justice,' said Letitia.

'I've been trying to read it,' said Dorothy. 'It's much harder to read a real French book than do exercises in class. As far as I can make out, it's about a thief on board a ship. Can't see how that helps with this mystery.'

'Keep reading,' said Justice. 'I'll write to Dad's scary secretary, Miss Lewis, and see if she knows anything. And I'll tell Henry to tail Mr Hoffman. Just in case.'

Justice managed to get a message to Henry the next morning. She was walking back from the gardens with a trug full of carrots when the St Wilfred's boys jogged past on their way to football practice. Henry was lagging behind, obviously dreading the game ahead.

'Psst,' said Justice, from behind the hen coop.

'Jones!' Henry stopped immediately. 'What's going on? How are you? I was so sorry when I heard . . .' He stopped, looking embarrassed.

Justice was used to this. People just didn't know what to say about Dad. Only the Find Herbert Group took the right approach because they treated it like a mystery.

'I'm all right,' said Justice. 'We've got a few clues. I can't tell you now, but can you keep an eye on Mr Hoffman?'

'Do you think he's involved?' Henry's eyes were huge behind his glasses.

Justice hesitated. When Stella had told her about her conversation with the St Wilfred's master, she had felt a bit guilty about suspecting him just because she'd heard him speaking German. Justice remembered what Dorothy had told her about someone spitting at Mr Hoffman in the street. It was pretty awful to be an exile from your homeland but still be suspected because that was where you came from. She didn't really think Mr Hoffman was a spy. But, on the other hand, she didn't want to rule anyone out.

'Just in case,' she said.

'Anderson!' bellowed the major from the front of the line. 'Get a move on!'

'I've got to go,' said Henry. 'But I'll keep watching. You can rely on me.' And he trotted off, looking like he was going to the gallows.

Justice wrote to Miss Lewis in evening prep.

Dear Miss Lewis,
I know you'll have heard about Dad. I'm convinced that he's been kidnapped and that he's still in Kent. Dad always says you are his right hand woman . . .

She paused, because Dad also said that Miss Lewis was a dragon. But there was no harm in flattering her.

. . . so I wondered if you could tell me who he's been in contact with recently, especially if it's anyone new, or with a connection to Kent or Belgium.
I hope you are well.
  Yours sincerely,
  Justice Jones

She reread the letter. It wasn't quite right, somehow, but she didn't know how to make it better. She put it in an envelope. As she did so, the door opened and Dorothy came in. Everyone stood up, just as if she were a teacher. Dorothy motioned them to sit down and spoke quietly to the prefect on duty.

'Justice Jones,' said the prefect. 'The head girl wants to talk to you.'

Justice stood up immediately. Letitia gave her a wink as she passed.

Out in the corridor, Dorothy said, 'I think I've got another clue. Let's go up to my room.' She held up a paper bag. 'I've got rock cakes from Mum.'

In Dorothy's room, eating the delicious cakes, Justice felt almost content. Rain was lashing against the windows but she was safely inside, and Dorothy had a clue. Then she thought about Dad and her happiness dissolved. She put her half-eaten cake to one side.

'What have you discovered?'

'I went home for tea today,' said Dorothy. 'Miss de Vere said I could because I didn't go on Sunday.' Justice realised that Dorothy had stayed at the school for her sake and she felt touched. 'I wanted to check that John got Sinbad back to the farm.'

'Did he?'

'Yes. Apparently, the farmer didn't even notice that he was gone. Anyway, Dad came in for tea and he told me something interesting that happened in the pub on Saturday night.'

'I didn't know pubs were still open.'

'The Old Ship is, but they don't serve spirits any more. Major Hammond was there and apparently he got quite angry about it. Dad said he used a swear word. People were shocked because the vicar and the verger were at the next table.'

'I bet no one asked the major if he knew there was a war on.'

'I bet they didn't. Anyway, people started to talk about your dad . . .' Dorothy stopped as she caught sight of Justice's face. 'I'm sorry, but everyone always knows everyone else's business in the village. Anyway, one of the fishermen – he's called Davy but everyone calls him Kipper – said that he'd seen a boat going out to sea on Friday night. There was a full moon and fishermen often go out then. But what was odd was that there were two men on board, and they were both strangers.'

She looked at Justice as if she'd realise the importance of this.

'So what?' said Justice. She was feeling sad again. Dorothy's clue had turned out to be just some pub gossip. Would she ever see her dad again?

'Don't you see?' said Dorothy. 'There *are* no strangers round here. All the fishermen know each other. What if one of those men was your dad?'

Dad had disappeared late on Friday afternoon. Had he been taken somewhere by boat that evening?

Justice didn't know if Dorothy's clue made her feel worse or better.

Back in the dormy, Justice wrote in her journal:

> Places to look for Dad
> Airports. Headcorn. Are there any others
> Places between Highbury House and London. Did he stop on the way home?
> The sea.

What would Leslie Light say about that? 'Be specific,' he always told Bertram the butler, who sometimes helped on his cases. You couldn't get less specific than a whole ocean.

Justice wrote:

Was Dad on that boat? If so, where were they taking him?

All the way to France? And why was Bessie left at Headcorn? As a red herring?

Red herrings, a fisherman called Kipper – it was all getting very strange. Fishy, in fact.

She added: *Who drove Bessie? Look out for someone with short legs.*

This last was so ridiculous that Justice almost laughed aloud. But writing the list made her feel slightly better. She'd solved other cases. Surely she could solve this one. What did Leslie Light always say? *Assemble the facts and look for a pattern.*

'Justice!' hissed Rose. 'I can see your torch light. We're meant to have a blackout.'

Justice turned off her torch. She could think just as well in the dark.

Assemble the facts and look for a pattern.

Dad was involved in espionage work. Espionage means spying.

Dad drove to see me for the half holiday on Friday 20 October. He left at approximately 6 p.m.

He never got home. His car was found at Headcorn airport on Saturday 21st.

A boat was seen leaving the harbour on the night of Friday 20th. The two men on board were strangers to the local fishermen.

Dad underlined the word 'Kent' in his Shakespeare book.

Who else was involved? Maybe Monsieur Pierre (RIP)? Maybe someone at Dad's work? See what Miss Lewis says.

She was trying to think of other facts when someone screamed.

It was Eva. She was sitting up in bed and pointing to the window. 'I saw a man's shadow! There! At the window.'

'Don't be silly, Eva,' came Rose's voice. 'We're two floors up.'

'I saw it! I saw a shape against the blackout blind.'

'That's impossible,' said Rose.

But Justice was thinking of the face at the window in the tower. There was someone in the school who apparently seemed to be able to climb walls and appear and disappear at will. She got out of bed. 'I'm going to have a look,' she said.

'You can't,' said Rose. 'We need to keep the blackout up.'

'There must be a moon, or Eva wouldn't have seen a shadow,' said Justice. She remembered Dorothy saying, 'There was a full moon and fishermen often go out then.' If there was a full moon on Friday, it would still be almost full tonight, Tuesday. She walked over to Letitia's bed, which was closest to the window, and lifted a corner of the blind. Sure enough, there was a lopsided moon rising hazily over the tower and making it look like an illustration in a storybook. The school grounds were quiet in the moonlight, a faint breeze stirring the trees. Was that a figure moving in the shadow of the gymnasium? It was moving strangely, bent almost double. Then a cloud crossed the sky and it was too dark to see.

'Justice,' said Rose. 'Put the blind back.' She didn't sound as cross as usual, though. She was obviously still trying to Be Nice To Justice.

Eva was sobbing. Nora was saying something about the ghost of Grace Highbury. But Justice was sure that she hadn't seen a ghost.

She had seen a spy.

CHAPTER 18

Justice was glad that the fifth formers were still on gardening duty. They set out before breakfast, walking over the frosty grass, to pick carrots. The vegetable garden was in the old tennis court, which was next to the gymnasium, which was where Justice had seen the mysterious figure last night. Behind her, Rose was complaining loudly.

'My feet are freezing. I'll get chilblains. My mater says I have to be very careful. I've got a sensitive chest too.'

'I've got sensitive ears,' said Letitia. 'And you're hurting them.'

The pumpkins looked bigger than ever, glowing in the morning sunshine.

'We could decorate them for Halloween,' said Eva.

'Decorate pumpkins?' said Rose. 'I think you're bats, Eva.'

'Thank you,' said Eva. This simple reply had the effect of silencing Rose completely.

Justice walked around to the back of the tennis court. Were there footprints in the frost? She thought so. They were oddly spaced and looked smaller than Hutchins's huge, steel-tipped boots.

'What are you doing, Justice?' said Rose. 'We're meant to be picking carrots. We'll all look like carrots soon, the amount we're eating.'

'I'd love to be orange,' said Eva dreamily.

'I'm just looking at the house,' said Justice. 'That's where Eva saw the shadow last night. If it was at our window, maybe it was trying to get into the rooms below.'

She could see their dormy: the window, like all the others on that floor, was half open (fresh air again). Below them were the classrooms that had become the boys' dormitories. Their windows were all shut. The walls were brick, slightly uneven in places. There was a drainpipe, but that was at the far end of the house, well away from the Barnowls' window. Could someone have scaled the wall, using the uneven bricks as footholds? Maybe it was possible. But why?

'Don't remind me,' said Eva. 'I'm sure it was the ghost of Grace Highbury.'

According to school legend, Grace Highbury was a

young woman who had been locked up in the tower and left to die. Her spirit was meant to haunt the grounds. Nora was collecting eggs with Stella, otherwise Justice was sure that she would have reminded Eva that Grace concentrated on weeping and wailing. She didn't climb walls.

'What's the window below ours?' said Justice.

'One of the boys' dormies,' said Rose. 'Carrington says his is the second room along. That window must be the last.'

The last room. The place where the wireless had been playing on its own.

At breakfast Justice received a tuck box from Peter's family and a note from Dorothy. Although the other Barnowls were looking hungrily at the food, she read the note first.

Got permission for you to come to my house for tea tonight. We can interrogate Kipper!

Justice smiled at 'interrogate'. Dorothy would never write anything as tame as 'ask questions'. Also, she still couldn't get used to a man being called Kipper. Justice wondered whether it would make her sad to see Dorothy's father, William, a big man who said little but was a very reassuring presence. But she decided that nothing could make her feel worse about Dad, and that seeing Dorothy's family might actually make her feel better.

They set out after lessons. 'Oh, no,' said Eva, 'you'll miss Meal.'

'I hope so,' Justice replied. She still remembered the wonderful tea she'd had the first time she visited the Smith family. Of course there was a war on now but anything, even the swill the pigs ate, would taste better than Cook's cooking.

It was almost dark by the time that they reached the little harbour but the fishermen were still there, pulling their boats up onto the pebbles above the tide line. A sharp wind was blowing and it made Justice's eyes sting. Seagulls were swooping low over the beach, hoping for scraps of fish. The sea seemed to glow in the twilight, white waves breaking on the black shore. Justice thought of her father being taken over the sea in one of these little boats. What if it had capsized and been lost for ever beneath the water? Her eyes watered again.

Dorothy approached one of the fishermen, a wiry-looking individual in a woolly hat.

'Excuse me, are you Kip— Davy?'

'Might be,' said the man, who had a strong Kentish accent.

Dorothy took this to mean 'yes'. 'We heard that you saw two men going out in a boat on Friday night.'

'Might have.'

'My friend, Justice' – Dorothy beckoned Justice closer – 'her dad's gone missing, and we thought . . . we thought it might be him.'

Davy looked at them for a long moment, a clay pipe sticking out of the corner of his mouth. When he spoke, he didn't remove the pipe. 'You're William Smith's little girl, are you?'

'Yes,' said Dorothy, who was a head taller than the fisherman.

'Well, I'll tell you what I haven't told anyone else.'

Dorothy and Justice edged closer.

'It weren't two men. I'd stake my life it were a man and a woman.'

'We should tell Inspector Deacon,' said Justice, as they walked up the steps from the harbour. 'I'll ask Miss de Vere if I can use the school telephone when I get back.'

'You can telephone from The Old Ship,' said Dorothy.

'We can't go in a pub on our own, can we?' said Justice.

'It's shut now,' said Dorothy. 'I'll knock on the door and ask.'

Justice was sure they wouldn't be allowed to use the telephone but, when the door was finally opened, the landlord asked the same question as the fisherman: 'Are you William Smith's girl?'

'Yes,' said Dorothy. 'It's terribly urgent.'

'Come in then.'

Justice went into the beer-scented bar and dialled Inspector Deacon's number. In a very short time, she heard the detective's reassuring growl.

'Justice. What's up?'

Justice told him about the boat. 'The fisherman said it was two men, strangers, but now he says it was a man and a woman. I thought maybe it could be . . . it could be connected with Dad.' She heard her voice trailing away.

Inspector Deacon didn't say that she was wasting his time. He didn't say that her dad was probably in another country by now. Or worse. He didn't tell her to go back to school and leave crime-solving to the professionals. He listened in silence and promised to send some men to investigate.

But, when Justice replaced the receiver, she felt empty and rather stupid.

'Come on,' said Dorothy, who was waiting by the door. 'Let's go home and have a monster tea.'

Even that thought couldn't cheer Justice up.

After all, she had nowhere she could call home.

CHAPTER 19

On Friday, Justice received a letter from Miss Lewis.

Dear Justice,

We are all devastated about your father. He was
a fine man. Please use the enclosed to buy
yourself something.

Best wishes,
Joan Lewis

Inside was a ten-shilling note, the most money Justice had ever had of her own. She knew that Miss Lewis was trying, in her dragonish way, to be kind but Justice felt tears throbbing behind her eyes. Miss Lewis hadn't answered her questions and, worse than that, she had used the past tense about Justice's father.

'Are you all right?' asked Stella. They were at breakfast. Girls with letters were reading them eagerly but a few were looking in Justice's direction.

Justice showed Stella the note.

'She doesn't understand,' said Stella. 'She just doesn't know what to say.'

'I know,' said Justice.

'We've got a free lesson this afternoon,' said Stella. 'Let's have a meeting of the Find Herbert Group. Have you heard anything from Inspector Deacon? About the boat?'

'No,' said Justice. 'We're just going to have to solve this case on our own. Let's meet in the barn later.'

Henry met Justice, Stella and Letitia on the way to the Old Barn. Dorothy couldn't come because she was studying French. As there was now no teacher for this subject, she had to listen to recorded lessons on the wireless. Justice wondered if she was thinking about Monsieur Pierre and Arsène Lupin.

It was a grey day and the crows were cawing in the trees. As they walked across the grass, kicking their way through the fallen leaves, they could hear shouts from the playing field where the boys were playing rugby and, from the school, the discordant sounds of the orchestra playing Schubert's 'Marche Militaire'.

'How did you get out of rugby?' Letitia asked Henry.

'Asthma,' said Henry. 'It's very useful sometimes.'

'My brother Josh has asthma,' said Stella. 'He says it's horrid. As if you can't breathe.'

'A proper attack is horrid,' said Henry. 'But today I'm just suffering from not wanting to do sport.'

'I suffer from that all the time,' said Justice.

'Haven't things got better now you're a rounders hero?' Stella grinned.

'A bit better,' said Henry. 'With some of the other boys, at least. But Carrington is still furious because I got him out.'

'That was some catch,' said Letitia.

'Pure fluke,' said Henry. But Justice thought he sounded pleased, all the same.

In the barn, they arranged the hay bales in a circle and Justice produced some biscuits from Peter's parents' tuck box. Henry ate hungrily. Food was even worse for the boys because they weren't allowed tuck. Henry said that the term before, someone had even tried eating caterpillars.

While they munched, Justice told Henry about the trip to Headcorn, the *Complete Works of Shakespeare* and her sudden realisation about Kent.

'I'm sure that's what Dad was trying to tell me. That he's still in Kent.'

'Where in Kent, though?' said Henry.

'Well, I think he might be by the coast because a fisherman saw a boat going out to sea on the Friday Dad disappeared.'

'I thought you said it was a man and a woman in the boat,' said Letitia.

'The fisherman could have got it wrong,' said Justice. She didn't like to be reminded of this. 'After all, it was dark.' *There was a full moon, though,* said a voice in her head.

'Where could the boat have been going?' asked Henry.

'I don't know,' said Justice. 'I keep thinking about going to that pub with Dad on the half holiday. The Singing Sands. The landlord said something about the Kent coast. Dad said, "The seas are rough" and the landlord replied, "But the harbours are safe."'

'What an odd thing to say,' said Henry.

'I know,' said Justice. 'That's why I remembered it. But the boat must have been sailing to a harbour. What are the harbours in Kent?'

'Dover?' said Stella. 'Folkestone? I think my parents sailed to France from Dover once.'

'There used to be a port at Rye,' said Letitia. 'In medieval times. Miss Hunting told me.'

'Rye is in Sussex,' said Stella. 'There's still a harbour though. A ship ran aground there ten years ago. The lifeboat went out to save them but everyone on board was drowned. I remember being taken to see the monument when I was a first year at Highbury.'

A shiver seemed to run though the barn, riffling the hay on the floor. Justice began to realise how cold she was.

Henry said, 'I've been trying to follow Mr Hoffman. I think he's noticed. He called me his shadow yesterday.'

'Anything suspicious?' said Justice.

'He listens to music a lot,' said Henry. 'Old Hammy gets cross because he's always hogging the wireless.'

'Talking of the wireless,' said Justice. 'There's one in the last of your dormitories. Remember? I told you I'd heard it playing one day.'

'Oh, yes,' said Henry. 'That belongs to Old Hammy. He uses it for long-distance science lessons. We listen to some old scientist in Cambridge. None of us can understand anything he says.'

'Eva saw something strange on Monday night,' said

Justice. She told Henry about the shadow at the window and the figure she had seen hiding behind the gymnasium.

'Gosh! How terrifying,' said Henry. 'Did you think it was the ghost girl?' Justice had already told Henry the story of Grace Highbury.

'Eva did, of course. But I think it was the same person that we saw in the window of the North Turret. And I was wondering if they were trying to get into the room below ours. The one with the wireless in it.'

'Why, though?' said Henry.

'I don't know,' said Justice. 'I don't know anything.' Frustration bubbled up inside her. She had no real idea what had happened to Dad. She might be wrong about the Kent clue. He could be thousands of miles away across the sea. He could be . . .

No, she wouldn't think that.

She realised that everyone was looking at her sympathetically, as if they knew what she was thinking.

'We're making progress, Jones,' said Henry. 'We've got lots of clues. Old Spider Man is one of them.'

'Spider Man,' said Justice. 'That's a good name for him. It reminds me of that bit in *Dracula* where he climbs up the wall of the castle.'

'I've never read *Dracula*,' said Henry. 'Far too scary for

me.' He paused, thinking. 'We need to find a way to search places in Kent. Perhaps we could get the teachers to take us on a trip somewhere. Canterbury, maybe. There's a cathedral there. Teachers always like cathedrals.'

'They'll just say, "There's a war on, you know",' said Justice. 'But it's an idea.'

By now, they were so cold that they had to move. They made their way back to the house, jogging to get the circulation back in their legs.

Eva met them by the main entrance. 'Have you been out for a run?'

'Yes,' said Letitia.

'No,' said Justice.

'Oh, don't tell me then,' said Eva, and turned on her heel to go back into the house. Her voice sounded like she was crying.

'Oh dear,' said Justice. She hated to think that they'd hurt Eva's feelings.

'I'll go after her,' said Stella.

'I'd better go and pretend to watch the rugby match,' said Henry. 'See you later, Jones.'

Letitia went to find Miss Hunting and express a sudden keen interest in a trip to Canterbury.

Justice climbed the maids' stairs to the fifth-form

common room. There was no one there except Irene, who was knitting a jumper and listening to classical music on the wireless. Justice thought of Mr Hoffman listening to Beethoven or Bach and thinking of home.

Justice sat by the one radiator and wrapped her arms around herself to keep warm. Despite the meeting, she felt extremely low. It was a week since Dad had disappeared and they were no nearer to knowing what had happened to him. She sniffed loudly, and Irene asked if she was getting a cold.

CHAPTER 20

Justice woke on Saturday determined to be a better detective. On the face of it, the investigation wasn't going well. Kipper the fisherman now thought he'd seen a man and a woman, not two men. It was hard to think that Dad could have been kidnapped by a woman. Justice hadn't heard from Inspector Deacon but she thought the policeman might well have come to the same conclusion. They had got no further with their plans for exploring Kent. Letitia had suggested the Canterbury idea to Miss Hunting, the history teacher, who – sure enough – asked Letitia if she knew there was a war on. Justice didn't know if Henry had had any more success.

All the same, Justice told herself, Leslie Light would never give up on a case. He would look for the facts and assemble a pattern. And, because Justice's mother had invented Leslie Light, it was almost as if Mum was cheering her on. *I'll solve this case, Mum,* said Justice to herself as she steered her broom along the first-floor corridor. The fifth years were on dusting duties.

The boys' dormitories were deserted because everyone was at breakfast. Justice could hear the clattering of knives and forks in the assembly hall below. She could also hear Rose telling Nora and Eva how Carrington had told her that she looked like Betty Grable in profile and Veronica Lake from the back. Justice edged further away. She wasn't in the mood for talk about THE BOYS. She wanted to get on with detecting.

Justice stopped outside the last room in the corridor. This was where she'd heard the wireless playing. It was also the room below their dormy and so could have been where the mysterious Spider Man was heading when Eva saw his shadow.

There was no sound from the room today. Experimentally, Justice pushed the door and, to her surprise, it opened. She stepped inside. There was nothing much to see. Just a table with the wireless on it. The window was half open and the curtains were blowing in the breeze.

Justice dusted the wireless's wooden case half-heartedly, just in case anyone came in and spotted her.

It took her a few moments to realise what was wrong.

The wireless was warm.

As if it had just been playing.

'Maybe someone was using it for a lesson,' said Stella. 'Remember Henry said the major was using the wireless for science instruction?'

'It was first thing in the morning,' said Justice. 'All the boys were at breakfast.'

'Maybe Mr Hoffman was listening to music.'

'He would have been supervising breakfast. Henry says the boys throw bread at him.'

Justice and Stella were in the old art studio. It was Saturday afternoon and so, in theory, they had free study time. But there were lacrosse and football games going on, and the school orchestra was tuning up in the great hall. Justice and Stella had sneaked up to the attics, planning to say that they needed somewhere quiet to work. They had their Latin books with them, just in case.

Justice looked around the room, which had panelled walls and strange pointed windows. She remembered studying art there with Mr Davenport.

'*Just draw what's in front of your eyes,*' Mr Davenport used to say.

What was in front of Justice's eyes that she wasn't seeing?

'There's got to be something that links the room with the wireless in it with the North Turret – where Henry and I saw the face at the window,' said Justice. The art studio was next to the North Turret. It was another reason why they'd chosen that room.

'One's got a telephone and one's got a wireless set,' said Stella. 'Both ways of communicating with the outside world.'

'That's true,' said Justice. She remembered Miss de Vere and Monsieur Pierre using the turret to send radio signals when the school was cut off by snow. That was before there was a telephone in the room. Could someone be using the lonely tower to send messages to Germany? She was about to suggest this when Stella suddenly said, 'Shhh!'

Footsteps were coming in their direction. Then voices. A man and a woman.

'Is it safe?' said the woman.

'He said no one comes up here,' said the man. 'Besides, all the kids are out playing sport.'

'He doesn't know everything,' said the woman. 'I always got out of games when I was at school.'

You and me both, thought Justice.

'He should be here soon,' said the man. 'Have you looked out of the window?'

The footsteps continued again. Past the studio, heading in the direction of the turret room. Justice edged across the room. If only she could see who was speaking. She remembered the fisherman's words: *'I'd stake my life it were a man and a woman.'* Could he have seen *this* man and woman? There was also something about the man's voice that sounded slightly familiar.

Justice moved closer to the door and one of the floorboards let out a traitorous creak.

'What's that?' said the woman.

'There's someone in there.' Justice imagined the man pointing to the studio door. 'Let's scarper.'

And, before Justice could get to the door, the footsteps hurried away.

Justice thought about this conversation for the rest of the day and most of the night.

'He should be here soon. Have you looked out of the window?'

Who had then been planning to meet? Was it the man who had appeared at the turret window before? The Spider Man who climbed the walls at night? Stella said that she should tell Inspector Deacon but Justice didn't want to go running to the police with another false trail. She wanted to find out more first. She was sure that she'd heard the man talk before. When and where?

She was still thinking about it when they lined up to walk to church on Sunday. The girls weren't supposed to talk to the boys as they marched along the road but Rose and Carrington exchanged waves and soppy glances. Henry smiled at Justice as she walked between Stella and Eva.

'Church is super, isn't it?' said Eva, linking arms with Justice.

'If you say so,' said Justice. She wanted to be back at school with her journal, assembling the facts and looking for a pattern.

The walk didn't take long at the pace set by the teachers. The church bells were ringing when they arrived at the ancient-looking building, which seemed half sunk in its own graveyard, the tombstones looming up out of the grass.

The verger handed out hymn books. The girls were directed to the right of the church and the boys to the left. 'Like sheep and goats,' Stella whispered.

'A sheep?' squeaked Eva. 'Where?'

'Shh!' hissed Miss Bathurst from the row in front.

Justice opened her hymn book. She hoped there was something decent to sing today, not just dreary old psalms.

The numbers of the hymns were on the board. Justice turned to the first, number 205.

A small, handwritten note fell out of her book. There were just three words on it.

Veritas et fortitudo.

Justice couldn't believe her eyes. She gasped and, for a second, the church – pews, pulpit and dusty beams – seemed to spin around her.

'Are you all right?' whispered Stella.

Miss Bathurst turned round again. 'Shh!'

'Justice feels faint,' said Stella.

'Is this true, Justice?' said the teacher.

'A bit,' said Justice. 'Can I sit outside with Stella?'

'Very well,' said Miss Bathurst. 'But be quick. The service is about to start.'

The girls slipped out of the church just as the first hymn, 'Fight the Good Fight', started.

Justice and Stella sat on the low wall beside the graveyard and Justice showed Stella the piece of paper.

'That's Dad's handwriting,' she said. 'It's what he always writes in his letters to me. Truth and courage.'

'But how did it get in your hymn book?' said Stella.

'I don't know,' said Justice. 'The verger just handed it to me.'

'The verger,' said a voice. 'Don't you know who he is?'

It was Henry, walking towards them through the tombstones. 'I said I was about to have an asthma attack,' he said. 'It always works.'

'Run the straight race, through God's good grace,' sang the choir inside the church.

'What did you mean about the verger?' said Justice.

'I recognised him immediately,' said Henry. 'He was the face at the window.'

CHAPTER 21

'I told you I was good at remembering faces,' said Henry. 'As soon as I saw the verger today, I knew. I couldn't think how to get your attention, then I saw you going out of the church. I told Mr Hoffman that I thought I was getting an asthma attack and he let me leave.'

'Look what was in the hymn book the verger gave me,' said Justice. She showed Henry the slip of paper.

'*Veritas et fortitudo*,' read Henry. 'I wish I was better at Latin.'

'It means truth and courage,' said Justice, 'and my dad always puts it at the end of his letters to me. My mum loved Latin so it's a sort of link to her. It's a message from Dad. It has to be.'

Stella said, 'Are you saying the verger – I think he's called

Mr Bell – was the man who appeared at the turret window, three storeys up?'

'I know it sounds mad,' said Henry. 'But I'm certain it was him.'

'People say the verger was a trapeze artist,' said Justice. 'Perhaps that explains how he got up there. Maybe he was on a wire?'

'I thought that was just a school myth,' said Stella. 'Like Matron being a lion tamer.'

'I'd believe that one,' said Henry. 'Your matron is terrifying.'

'She's not as bad as some we've had,' said Justice. 'Believe me.'

'If Mr Bell put the note in the book,' said Stella, 'he must know where your dad is.'

'Yes,' said Justice. 'I need to talk to him. It'll be impossible now, with everyone about, but I'll come back this afternoon. I think he lives in one of the cottages on Dorothy's road.'

'How will you get out of school?' said Henry.

'I'll find a way,' said Justice.

The girls came streaming out of church, followed by Mr Hoffman and the boys. Miss Bathurst gave Justice, Stella and Henry a rather suspicious look but said nothing as they joined the end of the line.

Back at school, as the girls queued in the refectory for the watery Bovril that had replaced cocoa, Justice and Stella dragged Letitia into the hall to give her the news.

'You've had a note from your dad!' gasped Letitia. 'That's wonderful!'

'I know,' said Justice. It *was* wonderful. She felt quite giddy with relief. Dad was alive. He must be. But she also felt scared. Dad was in danger and she didn't know how to save him.

'Are you going to tell Miss de Vere and the policeman?' said Letitia. 'Inspector Deacon.'

'I want to investigate a bit more first,' said Justice. 'I'm going to see if I can go to the village this afternoon.'

She decided that her best bet was to ask Miss Heron if she could go on a cross-country run. That way Stella and Letitia, who were both also members of the cross-country club, could go with her.

'I don't see why not,' said Miss Heron. 'Take Rose, Alicia and Moira with you. Then you can have a proper team practice.'

Justice exchanged a horrified glance with Stella. 'Really? I thought it might be better just the three of us. Easier to concentrate.'

'I never notice you concentrating very hard when you're

running with Stella and Letitia,' said Miss Heron. 'No, it's safer if you all go. Just make sure you're back before dark.'

Justice hoped Rose wouldn't want to come. It was a misty afternoon and looked like rain later. Rose always complained that her hair went frizzy in the rain. But, to her dismay, all three girls agreed immediately and, after lunch, the six of them set off through the griffin gates.

'Now,' said Rose, 'perhaps you'll tell us what this is really about.'

'What do you mean?' said Justice. 'I just fancied a run.'

'You must think I was born yesterday,' said Rose. 'I've seen you whispering with Stella and Letitia. There's some mystery, isn't there?'

Justice looked around her but they were on the marshes now, nowhere for an eavesdropper to hide. She told the others about the note in her hymn book.

'Why didn't you tell Miss de Vere?' said Rose immediately.

'I just want to investigate a bit first,' said Justice. 'Have a look around the church.'

'Every time you investigate something,' said Rose, 'you always put us in danger. Remember Smugglers' Lodge?'

'That's not fair,' said Justice. 'I rescued you at Smugglers' Lodge.'

'After you'd put us in danger,' said Rose.

'Och, stop complaining,' said Moira. 'We'll trot down to the church and see what's going on. Nobody will be in danger.'

'Thanks, Moira,' said Justice. Rose looked as if she wanted to argue but, instead, she started to run, jogging steadily along the path towards the village. The rest of the team followed her.

It was raining by the time they reached the church. The little village was very quiet, as everything was shut on Sunday. Justice went to the wooden door of the church. It was locked but there was a sign saying: *In case of emergencies contact the Rev Percy Snodgrass, The Vicarage, or Francis Bell at No 5 Rectory Lane*

'I know where that is,' Justice told Stella. 'Dorothy's family live at number ten.'

She half hoped that she'd see Dorothy's parents in their garden or spot John going for a walk with his younger sisters. But the little street was empty. Justice and Stella walked slowly, looking for number five. The other girls had stayed in the church porch, sheltering from the rain, which was quite heavy now. The houses all had brightly coloured front doors but number five's looked faded and unloved. When

Justice knocked, flakes of paint fell to the ground. There was no answer.

'Let's look around the back,' said Justice. The cottages were joined together in a terrace but there was an alleyway – a 'twitten' the locals called it – that ran behind the back gardens. Justice was touched that Stella didn't protest at the prospect of trespassing. She knew that her friend was doing everything she could to support her, even breaking rules.

They found the pathway and walked past the cottage gardens. Most were very neat with vegetables growing in rows and a few winter flowers. Dorothy's had a swing in it. The verger's, however, was overgrown and untidy. An apple tree took up most of the space and the ground was thick with fallen fruit.

'What a waste,' said Stella. 'You can tell he hasn't got a family. My mum would have made pies with that.'

Justice's mother had made apple pies too, but she didn't want to think about Mum. 'Let's look through the window,' she said. Once again, Stella did not argue. They climbed the low wall and crunched across the apples until they reached the house. The window looked into a small kitchen. Unlike the garden, this was very tidy. There was a kettle on the stove and an upturned mug, as if the verger had just had a cup of tea. Face down on the kitchen table was a book.

'What's the book?' said Stella.

Justice remembered Letitia saying that not all books had clues in them. But this one did.

It was titled *Tide Timetables of Kent and Sussex*.

Stella and Justice ran back to the church, where the others were sitting in the porch.

'The verger's not home,' said Justice. 'But we looked through the window and saw a tide timetable.'

'What's so exciting about that?' said Rose. Her blonde hair was clinging damply to her head and she looked thoroughly fed up.

'It means he's trying to escape by boat,' said Justice. 'A fisherman called Kipper said he saw a boat going out to sea on the night that Dad went missing. That could have been the verger.'

'A fisherman called *Kipper*?' Rose was at her most scathing. Justice wished she hadn't mentioned his name. Or rather his nickname.

'The verger could just be a keen fisherman,' said Moira. 'Lots of people are around here.'

Justice remembered the landlord of The Singing Sands

saying that there were still fish if you knew where to look. Moira was right. Maybe this *was* another dead end.

'Let's look around the churchyard,' said Justice.

'It's raining,' said Rose, as if this ended the conversation.

'I know!' said Justice, wanting to stamp her foot. 'But there might be a clue. My dad's near here. I'm sure of it. He sent me that note. He can't be far away.'

The girls looked at each other, obviously worried that Justice was cracking up, but they all got to their feet. They went out into the graveyard. The rain was slanting through the stones, making it difficult to see.

'Remind me what we're looking for again,' said Rose, in a tone of exaggerated patience.

'I don't know,' said Justice, feeling the rainwater running down her back. 'A doorway. A secret . . .' She stopped.

'What's up?' said Alicia. 'Have you been struck by lightning?'

'A secret passage,' said Justice. 'There *is* one. I discovered it with Dorothy. It leads from Smugglers' Lodge to the church. It comes up in the graveyard.'

She started running though the headstones. Where was it? She thought there'd been an angel nearby or was it a Madonna? Dorothy would know but Dorothy was back at the school. She could hear the others behind her, Rose grumbling and Moira talking about the catacombs in Edinburgh. Justice searched on, peering at the moss-covered stones. *Dearly Loved. Rest in Peace. Asleep with the Angels.* A huge cross was a monument to, 'Thomas West, Who Died Suddenly'. A memory came flashing into Justice's mind. Wind, rain, the light from a torch illuminating a stone in the shape of a cross.

'It's here,' she said. 'Near this grave.'

The others came to help her.

'This is ridiculous,' said Rose. 'No one's touched these stones for hundreds of years.'

'Except that this one looks new,' said Stella.

She was looking at a white stone lying on the grass. Unlike the others, it was not overgrown and there was no writing on it.

'Let's try and move it,' said Justice.

'Are you mad?' came Rose's voice.

But the stone was quite easy to move. Justice and Stella managed it between them. When they pushed it aside, there was a wooden trapdoor underneath. Hands shaking, Justice pulled back the latch.

'Call the police!' said Rose. 'Dorothy's cottage is just there. Use their telephone.'

'They haven't got a phone,' said Justice. 'I'm going down. You all keep watch.'

'I'm coming with you,' said Stella.

Justice opened the door and shone her torch into the void underneath. 'Is anyone there?' she called.

'Justice!' came a dear and familiar voice. 'Is that you?'

CHAPTER 22

'Dad!' Justice almost fell down the steps. Luckily, she held on to her torch, which showed the stone tunnel that she remembered from that terrifying night three years ago. The voice was coming from her left and Justice saw that the passage branched off in that direction. She set off, Stella close behind her, and saw a barred window in a stout wooden door, and then a white face.

'Dad!' Justice ran forward and, the next second, was holding her father's hands through the bars.

'Justice!' Herbert's voice was not entirely steady. 'You found me. You really are a brilliant girl.'

'Are you all right, Mr Jones?' came Stella's voice.

'Stella too,' said Herbert. 'Is the whole gang here?'

'Just the cross-country team,' said Justice. She couldn't

believe that her dad could still laugh. 'Dad. What's happened? Who locked you in here?'

'I was on the trail of a group of spies,' said Herbert. 'They waylaid me after the half holiday. There was a woman in the road pretending to be in trouble. I stopped, like a fool, but before I got out of the car, I marked the word 'Kent' in my *Complete Shakespeare*, just in case. As soon as I approached the woman, two men jumped out from the hedge and grabbed me. They bundled me into another car. I don't know what happened to Bessie.'

'She was left at Headcorn airfield,' said Justice. 'Dorothy and I found her. We found the Shakespeare book too and I worked out the clue. Eventually.'

'Headcorn,' said Herbert. 'They must have been trying to make it look as if I was out of the country.'

Dad spoke in his normal calm voice but Justice could see that he looked tired and thin. His normally neat hair was rumpled and his chin was dark with stubble. It was the first time Justice had ever seen her father unshaven. She didn't like it.

'Did they hurt you?' she said.

'No,' said Herbert reassuringly. 'Francis Bell, the verger, brings me food and water. He's one of the gang but he's not a bad chap. He agreed to give you the note. No, the worst thing is the boredom. Nothing to do but sit and listen to the organist practising, "For Those in Peril on the Sea". We're right under the church here.'

'Who else is in the gang?' asked Stella.

'That's the frustrating thing,' said Herbert. 'I've never seen their faces. They wear their gas masks. I only saw the woman who pretended to be in trouble by the side of the road. I didn't recognise her.'

'Do you know where the key is?' said Justice, rattling the heavy lock on the door.

'I suspect Francis or another member of the gang has it,' said Herbert. 'You need to get the police.'

'I will,' said Justice. 'Inspector Deacon will come and get you out.' She hated having to leave Dad locked up alone in the dark again. *It won't be for long*, she told herself. *The police will come and break down the door.*

'Be careful,' said Dad. 'And put the stone back after you. If it's moved, they'll know I've been found.'

'I will,' said Justice. 'See you soon, Dad. I love you.'

'I love you too,' said Herbert.

But Justice and Stella were already sprinting away along the passage.

*   *   *

'He's down there,' Justice panted, as she emerged into the graveyard. 'He's locked in. We've got to get help.'

'Can we phone from the village?' said Alicia. 'The pub will have a telephone.'

'It's shut,' said Justice. She remembered Dorothy knocking on the door of The Old Ship. But Dorothy was William Smith's daughter. She didn't think they'd open up for her. 'Everything's shut for Sunday,' she said. 'Let's run back to school. Miss de Vere can phone Inspector Deacon.'

They closed the trapdoor and pulled the stone back over it. Then the cross-country team ran as they had never run before. Afterwards, Justice thought that their feet hadn't even touched the earth, that they had flown over the marshland, so fast that the rain didn't seem to touch them.

As they galloped through the gates, they met Miss de Vere walking with Major Hammond.

'Miss de Vere!' Justice hardly had enough breath to shout.

The headmistress turned, obviously angry at being interrupted. Then she saw Justice's face. 'Justice! Whatever's the matter?'

'Dad,' croaked Justice. 'We've found him.'

The others joined in.

'Tunnel . . .'

'Under the church . . .'

'Gravestones . . .'

'The verger . . .'

'Calm down, girls,' said Miss de Vere. 'And come with me. Please excuse us, Martin.'

Leaving Major Hammond – Martin! – staring, Miss de Vere led the girls into the school and up the spiral stairs to her study. Then she made Justice tell her the story again.

Even before she'd finished, the headmistress was dialling the number for Inspector Deacon.

Miss de Vere replaced the receiver on its cradle. 'Inspector Deacon and his men are going straight to the church. Now I suggest that you all go to your dormies and change into dry clothes. It will be time for Meal soon.'

Justice hadn't even realised that she was dripping on to Miss de Vere's carpet. They'd left muddy footprints too. 'I can't eat,' she said. 'I'm too excited.'

Miss de Vere sounded kind but firm. 'Nevertheless, you need to change out of those clothes. It won't help anyone if you all go down with influenza.'

Justice hardly knew how she managed to get changed. Her fingers didn't seem to work any more. Stella had to do up her buttons for her. The others were almost as excited. Even Rose didn't complain about her ruined hairstyle.

'We're heroines,' she kept saying. 'We saved the day.'

'You didn't even want to go,' said Letitia. But Rose pretended not to hear.

Alicia and Moira had gone to their own dormy to change but they met on the stairs going down to the refectory.

'Do you think the police are there yet?' said Moira.

'They must be,' said Stella. 'Oh, I wish we could know what's happening.'

Their wish was granted: Miss de Vere was standing at the foot of the stairs.

Justice knew by her face that it wasn't good news.

She ushered the girls into a corner of the hall to speak to them. A suit of armour loomed over them, arm raised.

'Inspector Deacon's men went to the church and found the underground room,' she said. 'But I'm afraid your father wasn't there, Justice. They must have moved him. The verger has vanished too. I'm so sorry.'

Once again, Justice felt the room spin around her. She had to hold on to Stella's arm to stop herself falling.

CHAPTER 23

'Inspector Deacon said not to be too disappointed,' said Miss de Vere. 'The important thing is, we know that your father is alive. And the police are on the trail of the gang. They are confident that they will find them.'

But Justice was sick with disappointment. She couldn't eat any of her food – not surprisingly, as it was the revolting junket known to the girls as 'dead baby' – and could hardly bear to join in the conversation around her. Rose and Letitia told Nora and Eva all about their discovery and their shrieks of excitement made Justice's head hurt. Yes, they had found Dad but now he was missing again and Justice had no idea where they had taken him.

Only Stella seemed to understand. She knew enough not to talk about it but squeezed Justice's hand under the table.

Stella also tried to change the topic of conversation but even the old favourite of 'I wonder what the boys are doing?' couldn't distract the Barnowls from secret tunnels and devilish spies. All the same, Justice was grateful for her friend's efforts.

After supper, Justice pleaded a headache and went to lie down in the dormy. She opened her journal and wrote: *Where are you, Dad?*

Yesterday, she'd got a map of Kent from the library. Now the place names swam in front of her eyes: Tenterden, Smarden, Ashford, Dover, Canterbury. Dad could be anywhere.

She gave up and, burying her head in her pillow, allowed herself to cry.

The next day was slightly better. It was always easier to feel more confident in the daylight. The Barnowls were back on cleaning duties so the day started with sweeping the corridors and classrooms. The good thing about domestic work, thought Justice, was that it stopped you thinking.

At breakfast, Dorothy handed Justice a note. *Meeting in my room tonight. We'll crack this case!* Justice wasn't so sure but Dorothy's optimism cheered her slightly.

The first lesson was English. They talked about

Halloween, which was tomorrow. 'Some people believed the dead walked on Halloween,' said Miss Crane. 'There's an interesting bit in *Julius Caesar* . . .'

The girls groaned quietly. The teacher was always bringing every discussion back to their set play. Miss Crane put on her 'quoting' voice:

'. . . *most horrid sights seen by the watch.*

A lioness hath whelped in the streets,

And graves have yawned and yielded up their dead . . .'

'What does whelped mean?' asked Eva.

'Given birth,' said Miss Crane.

'Golly,' said Eva.

The girls giggled. Letitia gave a quiet roar. Justice remembered the story about Matron being a lion tamer. If the verger story was true, maybe that one was too? The other lines made her think of the graveyard yesterday. *Graves have yawned and yielded up their dead.* The gravestones had yawned and revealed a secret tunnel which led to Dad. Where was he now? If only he could send her another Shakespeare clue.

'Are you listening, Justice?' said Miss Crane. 'What did I just say about Calpurnia?'

Justice's mind went blank. Who was Calpurnia again? Oh, yes, she was Caesar's wife.

'She was above suspicion,' whispered Stella. Justice repeated that and Miss Crane seemed satisfied.

But, in real life, thought Justice, *no one is above suspicion.*

Justice didn't see Henry until the evening. She was sweeping the boys' corridor, very slowly, hoping that he'd realise that's where she was. Sure enough, before she'd got to the stairs, Henry's blond head appeared above the banister rail.

'Jones! Hoped I'd find you here. What's been happening?'

'What have you heard?'

'Some very wild stories. That you found your dad buried in an unmarked grave. That you fought the verger and killed him. That Rose saved the day. That one was from Carrington.'

'I'll tell you what really happened.'

They sat on the top step and Justice told Henry about yesterday's adventures. Once again, he was the perfect audience, not interrupting but gasping in all the right places.

'So you don't know where your dad is now?' said Henry, when Justice paused for breath.

'No,' said Justice, feeling depressed again.

'*What* is going on?' bellowed an angry voice.

Justice and Henry jumped up and saw Major Hammond standing over them, his face purple with rage. 'Anderson, what is the meaning of this? Talking to a girl! Sitting and gossiping like a housemaid!'

There were lots of things Justice could have said to this. Housemaids were far too busy to gossip. She wasn't a 'girl'. Her name was Justice Jones. But, wisely, she kept silent.

'Anderson, you will report to me in my office tomorrow morning,' said the major.

'Yes, sir.'

'And you' – the major pointed at Justice – 'Miss de Vere will be informed of your behaviour.'

How? thought Justice. *When you don't even know my name?*

But the major seemed to have cheered up. He carried on down the stairs, humming a tune. It wasn't until he was out of sight that Justice recognised it: 'For Those in Peril on the Sea.'

'That hymn.' Justice grasped Henry's arm.

'What about it?' Henry looked upset, probably at the thought of Major Hammond tomorrow.

'No time to explain but I think Major Hammond might be the spy. Come on.'

Justice sprinted down the stairs, Henry behind her. She was just in time to see Major Hammond going out of the front door.

'We need to follow him.'

Justice didn't wait to hear Henry's response. As they pushed open the double doors, they could hear the dormy bell ringing. Good, thought Justice, everyone will be too busy moving around to notice their absence.

It was dark outside so fairly easy to follow the stocky figure as he skirted the house, walking in the direction of the pigsties. Justice could hear the sow grunting, but Major Hammond didn't look round. He was heading towards his car.

Justice pulled Henry back into the shadows of the house. 'Can you distract the major? I need to get into his car.'

'What?'

'Please, Henry. Just do it. I need to find my dad. You can tell Miss de Vere after I've gone.'

Doubled over Justice sprinted across the grass and positioned herself behind a hedge. She could see Major Hammond unlocking his red sports car.

'Please, sir?' came Henry's voice.

Thank you, thank you, Henry.

'Anderson!' Major Hammond wheeled round. 'What do you mean by following me? Have you taken leave of your senses, boy?'

'No, sir,' stuttered Henry. 'I just wanted to say . . . about earlier . . .'

Major Hammond walked towards Henry. Justice took her chance. She ran towards the car, unhooked the boot and climbed in. She pulled it shut, hoping the noise wouldn't make the major turn around. But, no, he was too busy shouting at Henry. She could hear words like 'insolence' and 'tomfoolery'. Poor Henry. She hoped that he would never have to have his interview with the headmaster.

Justice felt the car dip down. The major must be in the front seat. The engine roared into life and then they were bumping forward, Justice curled up in the boot.

It was only then that she wondered how she would get out.

CHAPTER 24

Justice tried to keep track of the twists and turns but it was impossible. She was battered from side to side, her head hitting the top of the boot. The car also smelled strongly of petrol and, before long, she was feeling too sick to think of anything. She was crunched up in a ball, her nose pressed against her knees. It was hard enough to breathe, let alone think. She had thought she might be able to listen for sounds that would tell her where they were but all she could hear was the noise of the car engine and, occasionally, the major singing a cheery song about a diver dying alone in the 'dep-ep-epths of the sea'.

Finally, when she thought she couldn't bear it much longer, the car stopped. In the sudden silence, she could hear the sea and the cry of seagulls. They must be by the coast.

The car door slammed and the major's feet crunched over gravel. 'Lucas!' he called. 'Where are you, man?'

Justice managed to wriggle around and try the catch. Thank goodness it worked from the inside. Very slowly, she started to ease the car boot open. Immediately, she could smell the sea. A woman's voice said, 'Martin! Is that you?' Justice was sure it was the woman she had heard when she was in the art studio.

'Who else would it be?' snapped the major. 'Have you got Jones there?'

'Yes, locked up in the cellar. Took Tom and two others to get him in there. He's strong.'

'Don't worry about that,' said the major. 'I've got a gun. Now go and get him, Lydia. Chop chop.'

Up until that moment Justice still hadn't been sure. But now she knew. Major Hammond wasn't just a bad-tempered teacher; he was a dangerous spy armed with a gun. What should she do? What if the major was about to kill Dad in front of her? *I'll have to stop him*, she told herself. *Somehow I'll have to stop him*.

Justice waited, listening to the waves and the impatient thumping of the major's boots as he paced up and down. Where were they? Who was the woman, Lydia? And who was the 'Tom' she had mentioned? The major had called the man 'Lucas'.

Justice pushed the boot open a little further. Now she could see a building and a sign creaking in the night breeze. The Singing Sands.

The Singing Sands. The pub Justice and her dad had visited on the half holiday. The place where they'd eaten fish and chips and talked to the landlord. It must have been the landlord and his wife that she'd heard that day in the art studio, Tom and Lydia Lucas. That was why the man's voice had sounded familiar. She remembered the strange conversation he'd had with Dad.

'The seas are rough.'

'But the harbours are safe.'

Henry had said it sounded odd. Was that because it was some kind of password? The fact that the landlord said these words had made Dad think they were on the same side. But obviously the landlord and his wife had been working with the mysterious gang who kidnapped Dad. They had betrayed him.

Next she heard a scuffling sound and Lucas appeared with another man. Between them, struggling hard, was Dad.

'Less of that,' said the major, 'or you'll get a bullet in your head and you'll never see your busybody daughter again. Get in the car.'

'Shall we put him in the boot?' asked Lucas.

Justice held her breath.

'No,' said the major. 'He'll never fit. Put him in the passenger seat and you get behind him with the gun. There should be room.'

'Why've you got such a ridiculous car?' grumbled Lucas.

'It's not ridiculous. It's a Fiat Balilla,' said Major Hammond. 'Built by Mussolini himself. Now get him in. The boat won't wait for ever. We have to catch the tide.'

The boat. They were taking Dad over the sea. But from where? Lucas had boasted about knowing the coast like the back of his hand. He might know all sorts of secret ports and landing places. Had Lucas and his wife been the man and woman in the boat? Justice remembered the book in the verger's kitchen. *Tide Timetables of Kent and Sussex*. She should have known then.

Justice had to stop them. She heard Dad saying something angry and the major laughing. Closing the boot, Justice clenched her fists and curled up. The car started up again. They were rattling over the uneven ground and Justice was more jolted than ever. Added to her discomfort was her increasing panic about Dad. How could she save him? If only she could let Inspector Deacon know where she was. Henry would have told Miss de Vere about Major Hammond by now, but would she even believe him? And how could

186

anyone possibly know about The Singing Sands? Inspector Deacon would probably go to Headcorn, thinking that they'd be transporting Dad by plane. How could he guess that the spies were using a boat?

They seemed to be going very fast in an almost straight line. She thought that they were crossing the marshes again. Then, without warning, the car stopped.

Justice was thrown forward, hitting her head on metal.

She heard the major swear. 'Tractor blocking the road! Probably being driven by one of those fool Land Girls.'

The driver's door opened. 'Give me the gun,' said Major Hammond.

'You can't shoot a Land Girl!' Lucas sounded frightened.

'Just give me the gun and stop arguing.' The major sounded like a teacher.

Lucas must have handed the gun over because the major got out. Justice felt the car shift and then rock violently. Dad must be struggling with Lucas. She pushed open the boot. She had to help. But, as she stepped onto the ground, feeling rather shaky, something burst into the light from the headlamps. A huge animal with a white face.

'Up, Sinbad!' shouted a voice.

Justice saw metal hooves shining and the major falling.

'Justice!' Dorothy and Henry were clambering out of the

tractor's high seats. At the same time, Dad emerged from the car, slamming the door behind him. There was no sign of Lucas.

'*Dorothy?*' said Dad, in amazement. Then, 'Justice!' as Justice flung herself into his arms. Justice's dad hugged her briefly and then said, 'What's happened to the major?'

'He's out cold,' said John. 'I've been teaching Sinbad to rear up.'

'He was splendid,' said Dad. 'But I think we ought to tie Hammond up. Lucas is out of action for the moment.'

Dad bent over the major, who was lying spread-eagled with the carthorse standing over him. When Dad straightened up, he was holding the gun. John was tying the major's hands with what looked like a rope halter.

'We need to get help,' said Dad. 'These two are dangerous spies.'

'I telephoned the police from a call box,' said Henry, speaking for the first time. 'We're not far from the village. I guessed about the landlord of the pub. That strange thing he said. I guessed it must be a password. I told Miss de Vere about you going off in the major's car and she rang the police. Inspector Deacon assumed he was going to the airbase at Headcorn so he went to intercept him. Miss de Vere and Miss Morris went too, in Miss Morris's car. But I suddenly realised that he must be driving to the coast. So I went to Dorothy and she got her father's tractor. We knew you'd come this way because there's only one road over the marsh. We thought we could block it.'

'Very clever,' said Dad. 'And whose is the charger?'

'He's mine,' said John. 'Well, he really belongs to the farmer. I'm Dorothy's brother.'

'You're all heroes,' said Dad. 'And where did you spring from, Justice?'

'I was in the boot of the car,' said Justice.

'The boot of the . . .?' Dad started to laugh and he was still laughing five minutes later when the police arrived, pretending that they were the ones to save the day.

CHAPTER 25

At first there was confusion. The two policemen didn't know what to make of the man tied up on the grass and the other man unconscious in the car, to say nothing of the horse and the tractor. Dorothy, John and Justice were all keen to add their versions of the story. Only Henry kept quiet. In the end, Herbert had to use his barrister voice to make everyone listen to him.

'These two are German spies,' he said. 'I'm part of an espionage team known to Inspector Deacon. If you convey them to the police station, officers, I will take these children back to school and then follow you.'

As if hypnotised, the policemen did as they were told. They got the major to his feet. He was coming round and kept saying things like: 'Outrage . . . headmaster of an important public school . . . taxpayer . . . make a complaint..' One of the officers said that everything would be sorted out back at the station. Lucas was dragged out of the Fiat Balilla and put into the police car.

Dad got behind the wheel of the red car. 'Hop in, Justice and Henry. Dorothy, will you be all right taking the tractor back to the farm?'

'Yes,' said Dorothy. 'I'm used to driving it. And John can follow behind.'

John was mounted on Sinbad again. As they drove away, he saluted them.

It gave Justice a cold feeling, thinking that John could be in the army and saluting for real in a few years' time.

It was eleven o'clock by the time they reached Highbury House, but as Herbert, Justice and Henry walked through the double doors, Miss de Vere appeared from her sitting room. 'Herbert! You're safe.' She flung her arms around Dad and kissed him. Justice coughed loudly and she let go. 'Justice,' said the headmistress, in her normal voice. 'Whatever has been going on? Henry said that you got into the boot of Major Hammond's car.'

'It's a long story,' said Justice. She suddenly felt very tired and she ached all over.

'I need to go to the police station,' said Herbert. 'I'll be back as quickly as I can. Is Deacon there?'

'Yes,' said Miss de Vere. 'When you weren't at Headcorn he went to the local station to ring Scotland Yard.'

'I'd better be off then,' said Herbert. He gave Justice a quick hug. 'See you soon.' Apart from the stubble, which was now almost a beard, he seemed his old self again.

Miss de Vere turned to Justice but, before she could speak, Stella and Eva came flying down the stairs.

'Justice!' Stella hugged her.

But Eva ignored Justice and just stared at Henry with shining eyes. 'Thank goodness you're safe.'

Miss de Vere told Justice to go straight to the sick bay. Matron bathed her forehead and said she'd have quite a bump the next day.

'Can I stay up until Dad gets back?' asked Justice.

'If you sit here quietly,' said Matron. 'Stella can stay with you.' Stella had refused to leave Justice's side. Eva had gone back to the dormy.

'Did you know about Eva?' Justice asked Stella when Matron was out of the room. 'That she liked Henry, I mean.'

'I guessed,' said Stella. 'She was so upset when Rose said

you were in love with him. And her sketchpad's full of drawings of him.'

'That's why she wouldn't let me look at it,' said Justice. 'I didn't guess at all. Some sleuth I am.'

'You had other things on your mind,' said Stella. 'And you found your dad. That's the important thing. However did you guess about Major Hammond?'

'He was humming "For Those in Peril on the Sea",' said Justice. 'Dad said he kept hearing the organist playing it. That meant the major had been near the church, probably even in the secret passage. Also, Major Hammond was with Miss de Vere when we told her about the underground room. He must have overheard and moved Dad. There was no one else it could have been.'

'Was it terrifying?' said Stella. 'Being in the boot of his car?'

'Yes,' admitted Justice. 'Especially when I knew he had a gun. I didn't know what to do. Then I heard the major saying that there was a tractor in the road. I thought of Dorothy at once. She told me that she'd learnt to drive on a tractor.'

'Henry and Dorothy went running off into the night,' said Stella. 'None of us had any idea what they meant to do. We all stayed up, all the Barnowls. We couldn't go to sleep without knowing if you were safe. Eva and I kept watch.'

Suddenly, Justice felt near to tears. *It's because I'm so tired,* she thought. 'You've all been great,' she said. 'I couldn't have got through this last week without you.'

'We're your friends,' said Stella. 'We care about you.'

Luckily, before Justice could start to cry in earnest, Matron came back into the room with tea and buttered toast.

'The last of the butter,' she said. 'Cook will be furious.'

'Thank you!' The girls started to eat.

'Matron,' said Justice, between mouthfuls. 'Were you really a lion tamer?'

'Don't be silly,' said Matron. 'I always worked with tigers.'

Justice was feeling very sleepy by the time Dad and Miss de Vere appeared. Stella was actually asleep on the couch.

'Don't wake her,' said Miss de Vere.

'She'll want to hear,' said Justice, shaking her friend awake.

Justice sat very close to Dad as he told them that he was a member of an espionage group trying to get information about a possible German invasion. 'Jean-Maurice Pierre was our man in Belgium. Someone informed on him and he was shot by the Nazis. Tom Lucas, the landlord of The Singing Sands, was meant to be on our side. He was watching the coast because he knew it so well. He must have told Hammond about our conversation.'

'Did you know that Major Hammond was a German spy?' asked Justice.

'No,' said Dad. 'We knew there was a gang of spies operating in this area. They were working out the best places for German ships to land and preparing to help them when they invaded. I knew that their chief was a pretty important enemy agent. We called him Agent X. But I had no idea that Agent X was actually at this school.'

'He wasn't at this school,' said Miss de Vere – rather sniffily, Justice thought. 'He was the headmaster of St Wilfred's and goodness knows how he got the job.'

He got it because he was a major and a war hero, thought Justice. She remembered Dad telling her that lots of upper-class English people had admired Hitler. The major, with his military moustache and loud, bullying voice, must have been one of them.

'I actually met Hammond at the school on the half holiday,' said Herbert. 'I told Dolores in his hearing that I was going to Jury's Gap. He must have decided to kidnap me on my way home. When I was driving home, in the rain, there was a woman with a broken-down car at the side of the road. I stopped, like an idiot, and they abducted me.'

'Who was the woman?' asked Miss de Vere.

'I think it might have been Lucas's wife,' said Herbert. 'I didn't recognise her at the time. I just stopped because it was dark and raining. I wanted to help her.'

'Being chivalrous is your weakness, Herbert,' said Miss de Vere, with a smile.

Justice decided it was time to interrupt. 'A fisherman saw a boat that Friday night,' she said. 'He said there was a man and a woman on board. That must have been Mr and Mrs Lucas.'

'I think so,' said Dad. 'Lucas is an expert fisherman. He knows the coast better than anyone. He probably used a boat to come and go. Less conspicuous than a car.'

'Why did they kidnap you?' asked Miss de Vere. 'And, having done so, why did they . . .' She tailed off.

'Keep me alive?' said Herbert cheerfully. 'I don't know. I think they hoped to get secrets out of me but, of course, I didn't tell them anything. They left my car at Headcorn to make the authorities think I'd gone abroad. They were planning to take me to France tonight. Maybe they were planning to exchange me for a spy on the other side. Or maybe Hammond was going to shoot me when we got out to sea and throw my body overboard.'

Justice didn't like to think about this. 'Just as well you

thought to underline the word 'Kent' in the Shakespeare book,' she said.

'I don't really know why I did it,' said Herbert. 'I must have had an inkling that something was wrong when I stopped to help the woman. I certainly never dreamt that anyone would work out the clue but I shouldn't have underestimated my clever daughter.'

'I would never have thought it of Major Hammond,' said Miss de Vere. 'I mean, he's an unpleasant man but he was a hero in the Great War.'

'He's also a fascist,' said Herbert. 'He's been in the pay of the Nazis for a long time.'

Stella said, 'Mr Hoffman's father was a hero in that war too. On the German side.'

Miss de Vere did not sound surprised. 'Yes, I've had lots of interesting chats with Stefan. He reminds me of Jean-Maurice in a way.'

Miss de Vere had got on well with the French master, Justice remembered. She certainly liked to get on first-name terms with people. She'd even called Major Hammond 'Martin'.

'What about the verger,' said Justice. 'Have they found him?'

'Yes,' said Dad. 'He was caught trying to board a boat at Folkestone. He's informed on the group, which will be very helpful for the police. I hope they're lenient with him. He was kind, in his way. And he did pass that note to you, Justice. He wouldn't let me say anything about where I was being held but he let me give you a message to show that I was still alive. He felt sorry for you. He said he heard you crying in the barn one day.'

'I *knew* there was someone there!' said Justice. 'And I saw him at the turret window one night. Three floors up. I couldn't believe it.'

'Francis had been a circus performer,' said Dad. 'And he used his ropes to climb up to the tower. He used to meet Hammond there and in another room at the school. Hammond would leave the radio playing as a signal.'

'He must have swung himself up to the top of the turret,' said Justice. 'And taken his rope with him. Henry and I looked out of the window and we looked down. But we didn't look up.'

'Always look up,' said Dad.

'They were taking a risk meeting at the school,' said Miss de Vere. She sounded rather affronted.

'The school was where Hammond had all his radio equipment,' said Dad. 'I suppose it was safer than the church. The vicar didn't know anything about the gang's activities, by the way. Only the verger.'

'I heard Mr and Mrs Lucas talking in the school one day,' said Justice. 'They said someone – I suppose it was the major – said it was safe to meet here.'

'What impertinence,' said Miss de Vere.

'That's why Dorothy heard voices in the North Turret that night,' said Justice. 'And we heard the radio playing in the empty room. Eva saw a shadow at our dormy window. That must have been the verger trying to get to the room below.'

'Goodness, Justice,' said Miss de Vere. 'Are you ever going to stop playing at detectives?'

'I don't suppose so,' said Justice.

'I'm glad they did investigate,' said Dad. 'I might have known you'd be the one to rescue me, Justice.'

'It was team work,' said Justice.

CHAPTER 26

It was the last day of the term. As the war was still phony, everyone was going home for Christmas. The teachers had decided to celebrate with another rounders match: St Wilfred's versus Highbury House. The following term, St Wilfred's were moving to new premises: a manor house outside Rye. Miss de Vere, in her final assembly, had said that the two schools would always be linked, 'in hearts and minds'. Mr Hoffman had made a short speech thanking Highbury House for their hospitality and hoping that the rounders match would become an annual fixture. Mr Hoffman was now the acting headmaster of the boys' school and he seemed to have grown in stature.

Carrington was the captain for the match. Rose was captaining the girls' side. 'Romeo versus Juliet,' said Nora.

But the romance between Rose and Carrington seemed to have cooled. Eva and Henry, on the other hand, were often seen together, occasionally holding hands.

Justice felt a little left out. After all, Henry was *her* friend first. But she was glad that Eva was happy. 'Life is just super!' she had exclaimed that morning. Besides, Justice was busy with cross-country running and studying for her School Certificate. She was looking forward to Christmas. She and Stella were going to see a pantomime and Dorothy was coming to stay. Dad had promised that he wouldn't get involved in any more espionage work but Justice was going to keep a very close eye on him, just the same.

After breakfast, the girls walked over to the gymnasium to get changed. Stella had a letter from her parents and wanted to read it on the way. Justice walked with her in silence until Stella said, 'Oh my goodness!'

'What is it?' said Justice.

'It's Josh. He's had his medical but they won't accept him for active service because of his asthma.'

'Does that mean he won't have to go to war?'

'I think so. He's very disappointed.' Stella looked up, her face wet with tears. 'Oh, Justice, I'm so happy. But I feel so bad thinking about all those other boys going off to war.'

'Don't feel bad,' said Justice. 'Just concentrate on being happy. Let's hope the war is over soon.'

Dad thought that the war would start properly soon. He knew enough about the German plans to expect an invasion of France in less than a year's time. And, after France, who knew? But Justice decided to take her own advice and just be happy, for that day at least.

As they walked across the playing field, the St Wilfred's boys were already in place, practising their bowling. Henry waved as they passed. It was a bright December day, the sun shining on the old house, ringed by skeleton trees. Miss Morris and Sabre were walking by the woods. Even the tower looked mellow in the winter sunshine.

The teachers were right. You wouldn't know there was a war on.

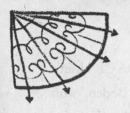
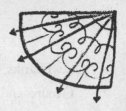

Acknowledgements

Of course, the war did not stay phony for long. By May 1940, France, Norway, Denmark, Belgium, Luxembourg and Holland were all occupied. When British troops were evacuated from the beaches of Dunkirk in May and June 1940, things must have felt very bleak indeed. History books will describe these events better than I can but, as the creator of these characters, I feel that I can tell you that they all survived the war and lived happy and fulfilling lives afterwards.

My mother's boarding school was evacuated to Somerset during the Second World War and they really did have to share their premises with a boys' school. My mother is the inspiration for Justice and, although Mum died in 2014, this book is dedicated to her and to all the children, around the world, who live through war.

Thanks, as ever, to my publishers, Hachette Children's Group, and especially to my editor, Rachel Boden, who encourages me by saying 'ha ha' at the funny bits but also shows me exactly how to improve the story. Thanks, also, to Ruth Girmatsion, Belinda Jones and Dominic Kingston. Thanks to my brilliant supporters, my agent, Rebecca Carter, and my editor at Quercus Books, Jane Wood.

Love and thanks always to my husband, Andy, and our children, Alex and Juliet. Love also to my school friend, Carol Dodson (née Haney), remembering the time we got stuck on the roof . . .

Elly Griffiths
2022

A GIRL CALLED JUSTICE

School is murder...
but she's on the case

**Missing maids, suspicious teachers
and a snow storm to die for . . .**

When Justice's mother dies, her father packs her off
to Highbury House Boarding School for the Daughters of
Gentlefolk. The transition is a shock. Are all uniforms such
a charming shade of brown? Will angelic Rose, her new
nemesis, ever leave her alone? And do schools normally hide
dangerous secrets about the murder of a chamber maid?

'Splendidly moody and twisty,
like *Malory Towers* but with added corpses ...'
Financial Times

**Justice Jones, super-smart super-sleuth is back
for her second spine-tingling adventure!**

When Justice returns for spring term, it's not long before
murder is back on her mind. Assigned to look after the elderly
Mr Arthur in Smugglers' Lodge, Justice is dismayed.

But dismay gives way to intrigue as she finds
herself drawn to Mr Arthur's stories of piloting in
the First World War – and especially when she
finds out that the lodge is haunted.

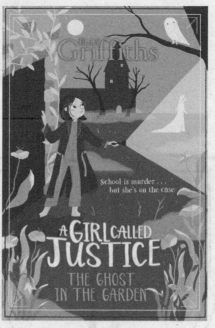

Justice Jones and her friends are third years now, and they are back to solve another mystery!

New girl Letitia doesn't care for the rules – and the teachers don't seem to mind! She decides that Justice is her particular friend, much to Stella and Dorothy's distress.

Then, after a midnight feast in the barn, and a terrifying ghost-sighting in the garden, a girl disappears. Soon ransom notes appear, and they're torn from the pages of a crime novel.